The Book

The Books of Magra:

Hax-Sus

(volume 1)

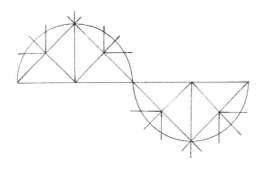

Joël Tibbits

JOEL TIBBITS PRODUCTIONS

Vancouver, BC

All rights reserved.

© Joël Tibbits 2018

ISBN: 978-1-9994090-0-5

    This is a work of fiction. Names, characters, places, events and incidents are either the products of the author's imagination or used in a fictitious manner. Any resemblance to actual persons, living or dead, or actual events is purely coincidental.
    No part of this book may be reproduced or transmitted in any form or by any electronic or mechanical means without the written permission of the Author, except where permitted by law.

Cover design and artwork by Joël Tibbits

www.thebooksofmagra.com

Contents

Part I	1
Part II	149
Acknowledgements	266
About the Author	267

In the Ras-Tor System…

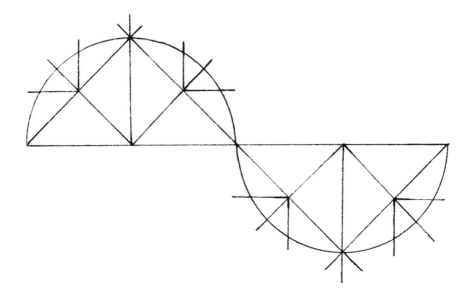

Part I

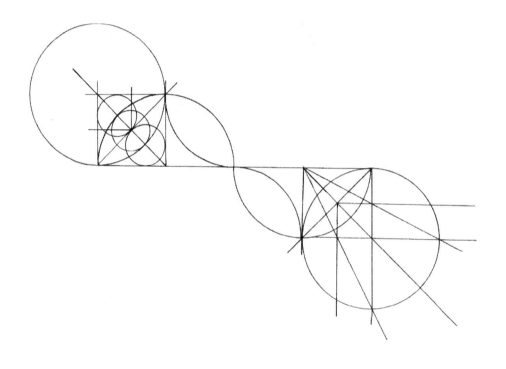

1.

The dark reverberated invisible depths.

The light scratching of paper drifted up to the roof of the tower as the boy squinted and strained to see those sounds within the dark above him. Head craned back, he watched flickers of light from the surrounding candles present themselves on the edge of that high dark; sometimes the sounds of writing would merge with the flickers of light and animate the fringes. They were suggestions of willful movement, of unknown life within the dark above.

But the candlelight never pierced the central pool of that darkness, and so the boy continued his attempts to penetrate the dark with what illumination his imagination provided. He envisioned the wood support beams, the nails and the copper shingling all arranged to form the conical roof. But he could see nothing but the darkness.

He had always marvelled at the tower's copper roof. It would glimmer in daylight and capture filaments of starlight at night. He often wondered what the interior looked like, but more than anything else, he wanted to know how it was possible to build such a structure, not only the roof, but the whole tower as well. The boy wanted to understand how you place stones one on top of another to reach such heights, or how you form the conical roof to such a precise point with copper. Often the boy had looked at the tower from his family farmstead contemplating its creation; it was a wonder he had for all the architectural marvels found throughout the kingdom.

  The boy's neck started to strain. He slowly brought his head forward; his gaze trailed through the dark and then crossed its boundary to the appearance of stones that formed the wall of the tower. Continuing down, stone after stone came into his view, each a little clearer than its predecessor, until he reached the top of the high bookshelf. From the top shelf he looked over the first book, then moving downward, followed a trail of varying spines: smooth, rough, thick, thin, worn and new.

  Finally, his eyes came to rest upon the old architect writing at his desk. He had thin features, his face deeply lined by time, and yet still emitting a youthful vigour. His long hair, grey as snow clouds, was tied back with tiny braids and draped over the dark blue-grey cloak that pooled around him on the floor.

  Beneath the boy and the old architect was a thick circular carpet woven with the most luxurious material and detailed with ornate symbols. The richness of the patterns in blue, gold, white and black complimented the symbols and figures with such intensity that the boy was struck with a sense of meaning emanating from the carpet. When he had first entered the modest space of the old architect's room at the top of the tower, the boy had come only to the edge of the carpet. He had dared not step into its lush vibrancy, feeling unworthy to step upon symbols that he could not understand. It was only because the old architect told the boy to come forward that he now stood in the center of the carpet.

  To the boy's left a large window as high as the bookshelf. Beyond it lay the kingdom. From his position, the boy could make out scatterings of firelight, but his reflection, and that of the room on the glass, obscured any other detail of the kingdom at night. Opposite the window, to his right, a drafting table covered with drawings that continued up along the wall. In some of the drawings, the boy recognized parts of the kingdom. But other images gave him no clue as to where they were, or in some cases, what they were. Along the circular wall hung tapestries with similar symbols woven into the carpet. A carved wooden door behind the boy and the smell of teak and tobacco complimented the air of richness and mystique.

The boy stood motionless for some time. At first he tried to maintain an unassuming presence, not daring to move, keeping his brow low and his hands tightly gripped in front of him. He did not want to interrupt the old architect. The boy watched him write, only looking at his old hands, never his face. At times, the old architect murmured as he wrote; the combination of his voice and the sounds of writing rose up to the dark ceiling.

Now as the old architect continued to write, the space above the boy became intriguing once more. Again he craned back his head as he followed those sounds up into the dark of the ceiling. Even though he felt very uncomfortable there was something tranquil in observing the ceiling and following the sounds of writing consumed by the dark above him.

"Come closer." It was a gentle request from the old architect but it still made the boy jump. The old architect did not look at him and the boy took a deep breath and approached. He stopped one step away from the edge of the writing desk.

Standing closer to the old architect changed things for the boy. The room became larger and its features became richer: the light given off by the candles, the presence of shadows, the contrast of colours, even the aromas were more apparent. The boy stood silently as his heart beat rapidly and his mind was full of thoughts. Am I close enough? What do all these shapes mean? I am so thirsty. Will he choose me? I wish I were sitting under my tree.

The boy looked at what the old architect wrote; other than their similarity to the shapes in the tapestries on the walls and carpets, the writing made no sense to him.

"Why are you here?" The old architect said as he continued to write. The words filled the room. The boy struggled to resist the urge to watch the sound of the old architect's voice rise up.

"I want to be your new assistant," the boy said softly.

"Can you draw?" The old architect continued writing, his eyes down.

"Yes...and..." For a moment the only sound was of the old architect writing. And then it stopped.

"And?..." the old architect's voice cracked and boomed upwards. He looked at the boy with a stern expression. The boy was stunned by the depth in the old architect's eyes. He scrambled to recall what he was going to say. He wished to find a deeper and truer response, something that would impress, but his mind was tumultuous with chatter. He found his way back to his first words but they were clumsy and inaccurate.

"…and…I am responsible." He chose his mother's words.

The old architect tilted his head.

"Truly." The old architect smiled. The word went through the boy and chilled him with its assertion.

"But you do not speak for yourself." The old architect's expression hardened and he returned to his writing.

The boy's heart sank. Have I failed?

The sound of the old architect's pen marking the page vividly rose and followed the sound of his words into the obscured roof. They did more than fill the tranquility of the room, they found folds and directions that saturated the air with the old architect's presence. The boy had never witnessed such a thing before. Everything the old architect did, he passed through. He seemed to make his presence move everywhere, through everything, without limit. The longer the boy remained in that room the more he felt the old architect all about him, and even passing through him. The boy attempted to pull away from sensing the old architect all around him, and the effort made him aware of his fatigue.

The boy had not slept in anticipation of this meeting. He had heard so many rumours of the old architect, and his sleep had been laden with the mystique by which people had spoken of him: that he was mad, a sorcerer or just quiet, but full of dark and unnatural thoughts. Some had said that he had brought to the kingdom, in his designs of buildings and engineering, what he had learned from dark magics from some far-off lands.

The old architect stopped writing and he placed his pen soundlessly into its holder. He sat with his hands lying comfortably in his lap and looked down at what he had written with an air of satisfaction. He took the page from his writing stand and placed it to the side, then looked at the boy and smiled. "Please, take my place."

The boy did not move. The old architect rose and stepped aside, gesturing with his hand.

"Please...take my place."

Still the boy did not move. He was confused by the comfort he felt. A warmth and encouragement rose from within the boy. It was somehow in harmony with the movement of the old architect's hand; an aged beauty and power accepting him. The boy looked into the old architect's deep eyes that captivated him. Even with the gentle and positive invitation the boy could not compel himself to move. It was all too overwhelming being in such a powerful place and receiving such a gracious invitation.

The old architect's smile and calm demeanour did not slip. The boy looked again to the guiding hand, and it was easier for him to move. He walked carefully. The carpet felt so regal and dense, each step felt as though he were being drawn into it. A sinking feeling filled his chest. His focus on the old architect's hand shifted to where the hand guided him, to where the old architect had sat. As the boy moved to the desk his whole body worked to hold the maelstrom of questions and thoughts in his mind.

The boy sat gently. There was no cushion and the floor felt very hot. The writing table gleamed with dark wood and the gold inlay from the pen and ink bottle shimmered. A new white page lay in front of him. The room seemed to change in its scope as though it had grown.

The old architect hid his hands in his sleeves as he stood just behind the boy. "Have you used pen and ink before?"

"Yes, once or twice," the boy responded.

"Pick up the pen."

The boy looked at the old architect whose face revealed nothing. The room began to feel oppressive and the boy became more self-conscious. What if I drop it? What will he ask me to do? I am so thirsty and tired. I should not be here.

The boy picked up the pen; heavy and of royal manufacture.

"Dip it in the ink." The old architect released a fragment of eagerness in his tone.

The boy did as he was asked. He carefully observed the pen's tip as though he needed to navigate it through unknown obstructions or move it in an exact course against vaporous wills tucked into the folds of the air. All of this while monitoring the clamour of questions inside his head and the confusion of comfort and intimidation in his heart.

The metal of the pen nib met the rim of the ink bottle in a sharp sonic colouring that broke the silence and so broke the concentration of the boy's movement. It startled the boy so much that he let the pen pause in the ink. With that sharp sound all the noise in his mind cleared and he followed the bright metallic tone up to the ceiling. He focused again on the pen and pulled it free when he thought it was amply coated with ink. He waited with the pen poised over the page, his concern to not to let a drop of ink reach the white expanse consumed his mind. He could think of nothing else.

"Now, draw a line," the old architect said.

"How long?" the boy asked looking at the page.

"You choose."

"In which direction?"

"That is also up to you."

The boy paused and wondered, Why does he want a line? Up, down, diagonal, which is best? Then he leaned in, careful not to make any mark other than the line the old architect had requested. Again, he dared not drop even a spot of ink on the clean page.

The pen was about to touch the paper. "Stop." The old architect said as his hand touched the boy's shoulder. The boy froze. "You may go."

The old architect smiled as the boy looked up in dismay and then fixed his gaze on the page. He returned the pen to its resting place and stood up. As the boy rose, his movement synchronized with the rise of a strange sound. It was an ascending wail coming from outside the chamber.

The boy was grabbed from behind, his feet leaving the ground as fire and glass exploded into the room through the large window. The uncontrolled movement of his body and the force of the blast felt as one. At the chamber's centre, embedded in the floor, now lay a great, black burning stone. Flames whipped and leaped off its slick surface quickly spreading throughout the room. The smell of some acrid oil had now engulfed the teak and tobacco and the boy choked at the intrusion.

The boy's shirt tore a little at the collar as the old architect spun him around and brought him under his cloak. The boy could see nothing and reached out with all the senses left to him. A burning roar punctuated with muffled concussions penetrated the cloak. The boy felt the velocity of the sounds as though they passed through him.

The old architect carried the boy by his underarms making the cloak drape heavily against the boy's face. It was a short-lived protective comfort as the cloak whipped back, revealing the door to the chamber.

"Move!" the old architect commanded as he pressed his hand between the boy's shoulder blades, shoved the door open and pushed the boy through just as fire consumed the doorframe.

The boy stumbled onto the staircase as the old architect held his collar guiding him down the spiralling steps of the tower. The fire followed them as the room was consumed. Burning fragments fell from the great rock embedded in the chamber's floor. Another explosion above, and the boy imagined the dark ceiling collapsing on them. The lower they descended the more surreal everything seemed. The turn of the staircase aligned to the spiralling of fear that filled his mind and body.

As they neared the base of the tower, the floor opened up into a large domed area covered with burning wood and chunks of stone. Screams and shouts filled the halls radiating out from the base of the tower. The old architect moved the boy close to the wall away from the cascade of embers and then focused on the center of the floor. *Why are we not leaving? What if the tower collapses?*

Just then, a middle-aged woman ran up to the old architect, crying and raving unintelligibly. The boy could not make out the old architect's words to her, they were strong and deep yet too quiet for him to hear above the chaos around them. Her eyes filled with confusion and question as three young children, a girl and two boys, clung to her long skirt, trying to stay within its folds. The old architect pointed at the children and raised his voice cutting through the sounds of destruction and confusion around them. "Go, woman!"

The woman flinched and she stumbled off, breaking the children's hold on her clothing. The old architect guided the children to the boy and they all huddled together.

"They are in our charge now. Stay here!" The old architect guided them to the wall.

The old architect was about to turn when he stopped and touched the head of the girl. "My dear, there is a way through."

Just as he turned, the boy saw a sadness in the old architect's face before it solidified into profound focus.

As the old architect moved forward, the children drew closer and pressed against the stone wall. He turned and paused. He measured the fall of embers and flaming debris then stared at the wreckage in the center of the floor which moments earlier had been the floor of his circular room. He raised his hands as he looked up to the base of the burning black stone high above. For a moment he appeared as a statute, motionless and unaffected by everything around him. The old architect slowly lowered his head and then his arms.

He stepped forward with elegant poise and without shielding his head, walked straight towards the center of the floor. For two steps he moved into a medium crouch and then thrust his arms forward. All the debris covering the floor exploded out, pounding into the opposing wall. He turned and opened his arms to the boy and the children.

"Run to me now!" They ran with their heads down, shielding their faces from the embers and shards falling hard around them. The boy, at the rear, glanced up at the chamber that had become as an inferno. It singed his spine and sent a cold, rippling mystery into his brain. The dark of the tower's roof had been swallowed and fed upon by fire, by voracious light.

The old architect encircled them in his cloak, the fabric cracked with the gesture. The sound of rock moving beneath them. Suddenly the boy lost his balance, then the cool dampness of stone as they descended a staircase.

In the dark, footsteps and breaths echoed through invisible dimensions.

2.

From above came muffled concussions of heavy impacts, screams and shouts intermingled with the pulses of running footsteps.

In the dark, the boy could hear the children panting as they clung to one another.

"Calm yourselves," said the old architect who stood just behind the boy.

"Where are we?" the boy asked.

"In the caves, just below the tower," replied the old architect. A deep boom shook the rock around them. Fragments of stone and dust fell and the children screamed. Their voices echoed through the caves and pushed back against the sounds of violence as their cries were swallowed by the dark.

"Quiet," the old architect hushed. Moving in close to all of them he said, "It is very important that we are careful here with the noise we make. In here, sound moves in different ways. I have spent some time in these caves. It is easy to get lost, there are many directions. It will be difficult to navigate especially since we have no light." Another heavy impact above. They all grabbed for one another as they stifled their gasps.

The old architect handed the bottom of his cloak to the girl and said to all of them, "We will make a chain, grab each other's collar or cloak." As they fumbled to arrange themselves the violence above resonated down into the rock around them.

"Do not let go, we have to travel in the dark for some time. Because we cannot see, it is very important that you listen and move with great care. Watch your steps and be aware of who you hold on to, and who holds on to you. Be careful with the sound you make."

The old architect took the lead, with the girl holding his cloak, followed by the others. The boy was at the end of the chain.

They moved slowly through the dark. Each step lurched with disjointed tugs from the links between them, uneven ground below their feet and the unending cacophony from above that reverberated throughout the rock around them. But even within the dark and stumbling progress between them, the boy could subtly sense the sure step of the old architect leading them.

Their heavy breathing, gasps and whimpers, discomfort and fear, and their footfalls bounced off the cave walls in irregular patterns, meaning that sometimes they were in tighter spaces, sometimes in wider ones. The high, sharp sounds made the boy feel cold and vulnerable, as though with every step he was moving out into a cold night.

The boy wanted to be the one holding the old architect's cloak. He longed for the security he imagined of being close to the old architect, and so the boy reached out for the sensation of the old architect at the front of the chain. As he was at the end of the chain, he could hear their sounds behind them and it felt as though the noises were absorbed into an infinite abyss. The boy felt so afraid and it was hard not to quicken his pace. As if those sounds would come back for him and swallow him.

The boy's foot struck a rock and it bounced hard off the cave wall. He listened to the sound dissipate behind him. He felt the abyss close in and he rushed forward. He lost his footing and let go of the garment he held. He fell through the dark and his hand met the cold hard stone with a violent slap as the sound shivered up into his teeth. They all stopped and held their breath in a moment of profound silence then breathed heavily again.

"Be light. Move carefully." the old architect's soft and direct voice inspired motivation in the boy. As he pushed himself up, unknown hands pulled him to his feet.

They continued on.

As they tried desperately to focus on their course, sounds came from above now and then. The boy gripped tightly the garment he held. Soon the stumbling uncertainty of their course became a flatter grade, walking was easier and the boy's mind flooded with images of the destruction that was going on above them.

He thought of the black burning stone and the darkened ceiling of the chamber. He imagined how the tower had collapsed and become a mountain of burning rubble. He could hear and feel the sound of the tower crumbling to the earth, its copper roof ringing a sharp tone as it fell and then silenced by the crush of the impact. His mind radiated out from the tower and envisioned the whole kingdom in ruins. The sights in his mind and the corresponding sounds of violence and pain shivered through his body. The boy tried not to think of his family, but no defence would subvert the images of his mother, sister and father. He could hear them crying out, begging for mercy, then their silence of death as their bodies, swarmed in fire, burned and cracked, lay consumed until ash. He shuddered and jerked the garment he held. The movement rippled through the whole chain, whipping back towards him and he fell to the ground. The other children fell with him.

"Watch your step!" the old architect whispered firmly to all of them. "Do not lose yourself up there." The children all lay for a moment, face down on the cave floor. The stone was hard and the sounds of violence above trembled through the stone and into their hands.

They journeyed on. The boy made certain to mind his grip and so direct his attention away from what was behind or above bringing all his attention into the rhythm and pace of the human chain. He imagined himself holding the old architect's cloak.

He recalled the brief sensation of when the old architect had shielded him underneath his cloak when the rock of fire came through the window. He rubbed the fabric he held and focused on the material as a distraction from the thoughts of what was transpiring above. The edge of fabric he now held was light, but he imagined the old architect's cloak: heavy, rich and valuable. The more he focused on the fabric through his fingertips the more he could define the fibers. The texture of each thread became more evident beyond binding material and assembling colours. He felt there was more depth in the fibers, more space. He clenched firmer trying to will the fabric to absorb him, and as he did, felt a greater connection with the chain he was part of. His own steps were more assured because he felt the rhythms of the others before him, and somehow, he felt they were receiving his movements.

They stopped, as did he.

"Wait here," the old architect said as the children huddled in around the boy. "I will not be gone long. Be as quiet as you can. Rest."

"Where are you going?" the girl pleaded.

"Not far, I need to ensure our route is clear."

They all listened carefully to his departure. It was a different experience for all of them. The sounds of his leaving echoed in the cave and changed not only the dimensions of his course, but for the boy, also the form of the old architect as he left. It seemed to him that the old architect had gone off into an infinitely expanding aperture. The boy wanted to go with him.

Shortly after the old architect left, the rumblings and concussions from above stopped. The boy felt an expansiveness to the silence of the dark in the caves; its stone walls briefly stoic before a barrage of heavy concussions trembled them once more. The children grabbed for each other. Anxieties and fears resonated so strongly from the children that the boy could feel them, as strongly as his own fears and anxieties. The boy was compelled to speak although he had no idea what to say. He remembered the old architect's warning of making sound and chose to stay silent.

He moved to the stone floor and the other children moved with him, huddling in the absolute dark. Their fast-paced breathing accompanied jarring and erratic sounds bleeding from above and travelling through the rock about them. Black thoughts coursed through the boy's mind as he fleshed out the sounds he heard; so many images unbidden. In the swirling negativity, the only platform of peace to rest upon was in sharing the sounds of their breath.

"At least I am not alone," the boy thought as he intensified his focus on their breathing. He worked to dispel the deep, booming violence above them.

Another concussion, the strongest yet. Debris rained down. They all cried out and the boy covered his mouth. How can I be careful with the noise I make? It is already noisy, what difference does it make? The frustration of it brought him to tears, but he held the sobbing in his throat.

Again the sounds diminished; again the dark silence of the caves. Their breathing eased and with the growing silence the boy began to feel an exposure to the dark itself. Whereas before, all the sounds were threatening, now the dark, in its invisible silence, was a limitless, amorphous, empty threat. The boy resumed his focus on the other children's breathing and pulled back from the foreboding dark to find a sense of calm. He was overwhelmed with the need to speak.

Very gently he said, "Are you brothers and sister?"

"No," the girl answered, "but people say that about us all the time."

"We will continue," spoke the old architect. His voice came out of the dark with such weight and direction that it startled the children and they gasped in response. The boy felt a rush through him and believed he saw a flash of light.

Then the old architect whispered to them, "We will go deeper into the caves. Let us resume our chain." He put the end of his cloak in the girl's hands. "Everyone hold on tightly and take great care of the sound you make." Again they navigated the dark; again the boy at the end tried to find himself in the old architect's cloak.

For some time things continued as they had been: dull and oppressive resonances through the cave walls; uneven ground of the cave floor; disjointing jerks on the clothing they held. As they progressed, the sounds from above diminished and eventually only the noises of their journey filled the caves. All the while, the boy maintained his attention on the old architect's cloak.

Then a change. At first a dim murmur, like spoken words, as though voices whispered from the rock around them; as though the dark housed thoughts. Quickly the murmuring intensified and the boy started to understand what was being said. Just as the voices formed a crispness of clarity, they flowed into a slim rush of water in a large space and the air cooled.

"Here. We are here." As the old architect spoke he brought them right to the edge of the stream. The water was rich with a crystalline reverberance that filled the cavern.

For so long it had seemed they were maneuvering in a cold, hard, black enigma; now the dark had a fluid form. The sound gave a sense of distance, of a greater space, and all the children realized their thirst.

They reached out timidly to drink. The first touch was a shock, an icy spike. They all lapped at it in small handfuls. They had to drink slowly as it was so cold it bit at their lips. Just the right amount brought tremendous refreshment, making them desire more.

The old architect helped the boy up and spoke to all of them. "Not too much." Then the old architect leaned in close to the boy. "Though I will be gone for some time I will give you my cloak. Cover yourselves with it and rest. Hold out your hands." The boy felt the cloak drape across his arms.

The old architect continued. "Stay in my cloak. Head and all. Tell the others. Remind them to be mindful of the noise they make. Stay under the cloak."

"Where are you going?" the boy asked.

"I need to ensure our route will be the right one."

"What if you do not come back?"

The boy felt the old architect's hand on his shoulder. "We will find our way."

The old architect left. The space around the boy shifted dramatically and some of it went with the old architect. It felt profoundly empty without him. He listened to the children panting and slurping the water.

The boy crouched down and spoke to the sounds of the children drinking. "Come here. We will rest under the architect's cloak."

The children came to him reaching through the dark. They fumbled into one another. The boy noticed that someone was missing. "Come here…" he whispered intently then realized he did not know their names. "Everyone under the cloak."

The other two boys moved close and they all went under the cloak and huddled together, the cloak enveloping all of them. The warmth came quickly.

"What are your names?" the boy asked.

"Myana," said the girl, then one boy, "Meneth," and the other, "Kalos."

"How long are we staying here?" Myana asked.

The boy was overcome with a paralysis to answer. It was only after he spoke that he heard his own words. "Not long, just rest."

The heat inside the cloak and their closeness kept the dark and its uncertainties at bay.

"Where are we going?" Myana asked, her voice light.

"Away from danger," the boy said, trying to find an answer for himself.

"I do not like the architect, he is mean," Kalos said, as he moved trying to find comfort, "The woman was nicer."

"Who was that?" Meneth asked.

"One of the maids from the outer halls," Kalos said.

"Why were you at the tower?" the boy asked.

Meneth answered, "She was taking us to see the architect."

Like me, thought the boy.

They were quiet for a moment and then Meneth spoke with a surprising calm. "I hope he is gone for awhile."

"Why?" asked the boy. There was no answer. Then the boy could hear the faint crispness of the stream. Someone had lifted the cloak.

"Why?" he said again, more urgently. The sounds of the stream were again muted and then Meneth responded, "I like it here."

Suddenly Myana turned and gripped the boy tightly, burying herself into his chest. She started to cry.

"What is it?" the boy said bringing her closer.

"I want my mother," she whimpered, her tears and sobs heavy. The boy held her and said nothing. He listened to her breathing, a compressed staccato. At first the boy was uncomfortable because she faced him. He could feel her breath mingling with his. He had never held a girl before. Only his sister had ever been this close to him, and she was older and would hold him. Then Myana's sobbing made the boy feel the need to cry as well. Thoughts of his sister soon shifted to his mother and father. He began to imagine all sorts of horrifying outcomes of the attack. He made great effort to stop what he saw in his mind, but the thoughts were coursing through his body. His stomach ached. He automatically brought his hands toward his belly, and so brought Myana closer to him. It was a torment-induced deepening of his embrace that compelled Myana to hold on and bring him closer. They stayed that way for some time until the boy heard a change in Myana's breathing. She had fallen asleep.

Now the boy heard all the children adrift in slumber; their breath calm and deeper now under the cloak. Their breaths formed a soothing weave of sonorities so different than breathing alone. Deep but also unclear. When they were breathing heavily because they were frightened or when they spoke, the boy felt he knew what was going on for them, but in sleep he had no sense of their thoughts or feelings.

Soon the heat beneath the cloak became too much for him. He uncovered his head and the delicate rush of water came into one ear, sharp and light. To the other ear resting on the cloak, the water sounded muffled and thick. He peered out into the dark, imagining what the cavern looked like, how deep the water was and how its ripples moved.

There was a pull to those sounds and in the dark the sounds had dimensions he had never noticed before. He felt an urge to go to them, to follow them, even interact with them. It was the way the sound of water moved and reverberated. Then he remembered what was transpiring above, beyond the cave and what the old architect had said about staying in the cloak. He drew the cloak back over his head and was again in a landscape of breath, its heat a discomfort, but it drew him from the painful thoughts and confusing sensations above. His eyes suddenly became heavy and the dark before him slid into another dark.

The boy had travelled for so long in the greatest density of dark he had ever known. With his eyes closed he saw sights he had never noticed or considered. Movement, swirling indications of depth, but he was too tired to comprehend them. The boy slipped into sleep.

All manner of dark softened and released.

3.

The sonic world of the cave came in like a rain of crystals.

"We must move," the old architect whispered, pulling the boy from sleep as he pulled back the cloak. The intricacies of its folds and spaces had weighed upon the boy as a great comfort. It had muted the space of the caves and softened the events above. He had drifted in and out of sleep, waking to the sounds of the children breathing, moving back into his thoughts and sleep's respite and dimensions.

The shock of waking brought the boy to his feet and he looked around, forgetting they were still immersed in an impenetrable dark. The boy turned and reached out for the other children. They were still under the cloak. He fumbled in the dark and rustled them out of the cloak's warm allure. Myana was resistant. "I am tired." Kalos stood up and yawned.

"Where is Meneth?" the boy said, his voice booming out over the stream and through the caverns.

"Be careful." The old architect placed his hand on the boy's shoulder and whispered, "Who?"

"Meneth." The boy crawled around on all fours reaching out and finding only fold after fold of the cloak. "Meneth is gone," the boy whispered. He stood with the entire cloak clumsily folded in his hands.

"Meneth!" Kalos and Myana cried.

"Quiet!" the old architect growled. They all froze at the sound of the powerful control of his voice.

The old architect brought all of them close together. Myana sobbed, the boy panted. The old architect put his arms around them in their small circle and spoke to its centre. "I do not know where Meneth is. As I said, sound is different here in these caves." The old architect's voice swirled in the middle of their circle, soothing. "We must be careful with the sound we make and it is better that we do not remain here too long. We must continue on." The old architect reached for his cloak in the boy's hands and drew it from his grasp. The sound of the fabric shifting and draping, changed the atmosphere between them and then it was infused with the sound of the stream's flow.

The boy heard the old architect putting on his cloak and took a few steps closer to the stream. As he listened his anxieties began to grow within him and anger emerged.

"We..." the boy began to speak strongly and stopped himself. He heard the old architect approach him.

"Listen," said the old architect. The boy heard the word rise and expand into the features of the caves. The sound of the stream grew from below. For the boy, it seemed as though the stream was beginning to flood and rise. A mounting pressure and strengthening of the currents filling the caves. The boy breathed heavily, his heart pounded. It all began within that single word, "listen" and now the boy was full of currents. They moved in different directions and rates. His thoughts flashed from one image to another. His emotions flickered in spasms. All these currents within, outside were pulling and pushing him. He was becoming overwhelmed with movements forcing inward, pushing outward, drawing in and repelling him.

The architect placed a hand upon the boy's shoulder, his voice very close. Again he whispered, "Listen." The same word brought the boy back from the waters of the stream's hypnotic movement. He felt he had returned to his own body. The boy imagined the old architect's face, wishing he could see him.

The old architect spoke gently. "Nature has its own rhythms, its own volitions, even its own appetites, yet we are a part of them as they are a part of us."

The boy spoke gently, "Where is Meneth?"

"Yes, where?" Myana whispered.

"I do not know. But I am certain we cannot follow. And we must keep moving."

The old architect put on his cloak and placed a portion in Myana's grasp. Kalos held Myana's collar and the boy took hold of Kalos' collar. They had resumed the chain missing a link, and so a rhythm, and a breath.

The sounds of the stream soon diminished as they moved on through the caves. The boy was eager to get away from the stream and yet he felt deep unease at the old architect's words. Not only in what the old architect had said, but how he had spoken. He heard fear and great uncertainty in the old architect's tone when he had spoken of Meneth. Now, as they moved through the caves as they had before, the boy's feelings towards the old architect were confused. Before, he wanted to hold his cloak and be close to the rhythms of his movements through the dark. Now he didn't know how he felt about being close to the old architect.

The caves began to twist and turn more and it soon became apparent to the boy that for the first time on their journey in the caves, they were descending. Their pace slowed.

The boy heard Myana speak. "Are we going down?"

"Yes," the old architect responded with a quick exhalation. Their words trailed off behind the boy.

"Where are we going?" said Myana.

"To an exit," said the old architect.

"Down here?" Myana said excitedly.

"Watch your voice," the old architect said gently, and Myana said nothing more.

As they gradually descended the air became cooler. It rose up from the deep and coursed over the boy like the breath of some unnameable entity. The boy felt exposed. As he was again at the end of the chain, the sounds of their movements and breath reverberated in the dark behind him. The sounds still felt foreboding, as though they would come back, changed and malevolent. The boy thought of Myana's words, "Are we going down? Where are we going?" And then his own thoughts continued. To safety deeper in the caves? How can we be safe when Meneth has disappeared?

Again the fear of being left behind overcame him and he bumped into Kalos. The boy whispered, "Sorry."

"It's alright," Kalos replied through stifled sobs. The boy wanted to know why Kalos was crying, and then he thought, Why wouldn't he?

Their route became steeper and the cave floor more even. The journey had been more difficult because of the ground's uneven surface. Now with a smoother course he was able to focus less on his steps. He became aware of the tension in his body, especially his shoulders. He was tired of holding on to Kalos' collar. It was a simple thing to do, to hold something, but in these circumstances it was surprisingly difficult. The boy wanted to stop. He wanted to rest. But the old architect said they could not. Somehow stopping was dangerous.

Meneth disappeared when we were sleeping, the boy thought. But what does that have to do with sound? Why is this place like this? Maybe it is not the sounds, but things that listen to the sounds. The old architect said nature has its own appetites. Maybe there are animals…or monsters down here.

The boy felt the emptiness behind him close in. He felt something pursuing them and walked quicker so he could be closer to Kalos. Even though he felt uneasy about the old architect he did not want to be left behind. The thought of being alone and lost in the caves of the dark terrified him.

The old architect stopped. They all froze and knowledge of the space before them rose up in the boy's awareness. Without warning, the cavern had expanded into a great immensity. They felt it roll out before them. The cool air was a fragment of a current from a greater source. The great space was in no way foreboding, but it was colossal. It felt as though no reach could know or define its dimensions. It was very different from the dark they had been travelling through with its continually changing dimensions.

The old architect turned to them, brought them close in a circle and spoke with a soft voice. "There are steps here. We will have to climb down." He took the cloak from Myana's hands. "On all fours, and on your belly or your side, stay close to the steps. Feel for the ground feet first, and make as little noise as possible."

How could there be steps here? the boy thought. How far down do we have to go?

"Is it far down?" Myana whispered.

The old architect continued. "Feet first, but let your hands feel the rock. Move for support, support your movement. Go very slowly." His voice was as the air, light and cool, but the warmth of the circle they formed remained. The old architect broke the circle and the boy could hear him begin his descent.

The boy heard the others follow. To find their way they had to embody every position of their hands and feet to find and follow the steps. Their movements on the cave floor echoed out into the great space beyond them. The boy found himself drawn to knowing what was happening with the sounds. They were resonating strangely.

"Stay together," the old architect said with a heavy hush. The words brought the boy back from his reverie of the great space and to the immediate need to descend the steps.

First he sat, testing the step before him, getting a sense of proportions and his stability. He turned on his side and laid over the rock steps. His breath came back at him off the coolness of the rock. The sharpness of the rock and the edging of each step pushed and scratched at his body. And yet, with what he sensed of the space out beyond them, it was a stable place to be. It was comforting to be in the caves with the security and presence of the steps. For the boy, it meant the uncertainty and wildness of the caves was lessened, because the steps had been shaped by others. And yet, why would there be steps here?

They had to go much slower, and so each step provided a pause. After the third step, the boy noticed how the sounds they made plumbed the depths around them. The body of each sound began so clear and sharp with a familiar momentum, but then they would move strangely. It gave the impression that the great open space was either a living entity or a profound neutrality, as though the cave were either some primordial leviathan devouring the sounds or an abyss without purpose.

As they proceeded down the steps they would often have to pause for the one before them to move along. They listened to each other, staying close. As the boy waited, he would leave one hand flush against the step and feel the texture of the rock. He soon recognized not only how smooth the steps were but how there were veined patterns in the rock. Each step felt as though they had been purposefully shaped, but the presence of the patterns confused him. If these steps were made with such care why would there be these rough parts?

"Stay deep within the steps. Feel the stone," the old architect whispered up to them. The boy heard his words as they curved out towards the great space the rock staircase bordered. The way the words had echoed compelled the boy to deepen his relationship with the steps.

As he moved from one rough veined spot to another, placing his palm flush, he started to recognize recurring patterns. It was not simply that the areas were rough angular lines, but the texture of the rough rock indicated some meaning. But just as he would begin to feel the forms reveal themselves, he had to move on to the next step. He could never get a clear picture in his mind, nor was he ever able to spend enough time from one step to another to create a connective meaning.

Step after step, the boy followed the certainty of rock that filled his attention, distancing him from the monumental space that pressed close. The pace gave each step an identity, as though it were a new plateau of discovery. He anticipated the finding and sensing of what each one would reveal. He wondered whether the rough textures were unfinished portions or were meant to communicate some meaning.

When the rock steps ended, the boy found his footing, inched his way down and was overcome by the openness of a smooth stone floor. All detailed sensations of the steps abruptly ceased and he felt a short burst deep within him; a fire that shot through him. His whole body became a flint, a flame, a furnace, then a sun. The sensations diminished quickly, enveloped in the cool air from high above him. He sat with Myana and Kalos at the base of the steps.

The old architect huddled them close. "We are at the bottom of the steps. I need to leave you again to check the way. Stay here, close together under my cloak." The old architect removed his cloak and guided them under it. Once they were settled, he said, "Stay together, be silent. I will be back."

The old architect's departure was muted, giving no clarity to his direction. The boy felt uneasy. He thought of the immense space before them and the steps behind him. He imagined its dimensions and tried to find a correlation between its proportions and the patterns of the steps he had experienced. He lay against the steps, imagining who might have made them. Why lead anyone here? He felt from that great immensity anything could come. His mind again started to shape gruesome creatures and hungry wills from out of that cold abyss that would devour them.

"I do not want to just wait, " Kalos spoke excitedly, his voice loud within the confines of the cloak. Kalos pulled the cloak from his head. "This place is incredible." The great space inhaled his words and amplified them. Myana moved closer to the boy gripping his shirt as she heard Kalos's voice penetrate the cloak.

"Incredible!" Kalos spoke again. There was a profound ease and joy in his voice. He stood up and away from the cloak. "Kalos," the boy whispered firmly.

The sounds of Kalos' steps reached out into the chamber as he walked away from the cloak.

"Kalos, come back," Myana whispered.

"Kalos, stay here," the boy said, pulling back the cloak. His words swirling around Kalos.

"This place is wonderful," Kalos said with a deeper assurance as his words rose higher.

Myana put her head on the boy's shirt. "I wish he would come back, I do not like it here," she sobbed a little. "It is scary." Every word she spoke hung within the folds of the boy's shirt and beneath the cloak, as Kalos moved farther and farther away. His voice and every sound of his movements had so many dimensions now, he seemed to be everywhere.

The boy wanted to call out to him again but he was afraid of what his voice might do in the enigmatic expanse.

"He is leaving," Myana said to the boy, "he should come back."

"H is alright, he will." The boy forced reassurance in his tone.

"No." the old architect said as he pulled back the cloak. The maelstrom in the chamber churned and roared in upon them.

Kalos' voice continued above them like an escalating chorus. His words and exclamations, after weaving and spiralling about, had begun to splinter into fragments. They became multiple layers above them, their distinctions intensifying, germinating, flourishing. Then they drew together in magnitudes far greater than his original voice.

The old architect formed a tight circle with Myana and the boy, their heads touching. "We must cross this space." He spoke strongly to carry over the power of Kalos' echoes. "I have encountered this before but not on this scale. We must travel through what Kalos' voice has become and not succumb to it. We cannot go the way I had hoped."

"Why not?" Myana asked.

"It is too dangerous, more than this!" The old architect shouted, his voice pulled into the currents of Kalos' contorted voice. "We must cross."

"Would it not be better for us to wait and cover our ears?" the boy asked.

"No, it is perilous to stay and we need to listen in a very special way. As we walk together we will hold hands and we will hum. Feel how the sound of your own voice fills your body."

"What do we hum?' Myana said.

"Whatever you like, whatever feels right. What is important is to feel it completely throughout your body. Keep your mouth closed, breathe through your nose, and do not stop humming."

"What about Kalos?" Myana said, her voice soaring away from her and out into the great space.

"I am sorry, my dear, there is nothing we can do except find our own way through." The old architect sounded mournful as his words were drawn up sharply into the maelstrom of sound.

"Give me your hands," the old architect said, taking the boy's and Myana's hand. The boy found the sensation profoundly soothing and he remembered the old architect's hand when he was invited to sit at the writing desk. "Walk lightly and do not let go, no matter what occurs."

The sounds Kalos had made were out before them, towering high above like a huge churning funnel. The old architect began humming a single deep, full note. The boy and Myana joined in with their own notes. At first it seemed silly to the boy but each time they hummed the sound became a little fuller and he felt more confident. The old architect took the first step and the boy and Myana moved with him.

Their first few steps took them through a sonorous curtain, and a chaotic movement like a wild wind moved through the boy's body. Immediately he understood the need to hum. Even though he had still not fully felt the humming through his body, he felt how it maintained a force against the turbulence.

There was nothing commonplace about the sounds. They all had different trajectories so the components, frequencies and harmonies would not retain the usual cohesion. As they moved further into the space, the sounds came in closer proximities. At times the boy felt as though the sounds were alive; as though they moved towards him with curiosity.

As they walked and hummed, the boy became more and more aware of how his humming tingled and ran through his body. Gradually, the sound of his humming filled his whole body and each hum no longer came from his throat but from some unknown source deep inside him.

The old architect's grip never wavered, never slackened or relented, but as the boy continued to hum the sensation of the old architect's hand began to change. At first it softened and then it disappeared.

The friction from the sonic maelstrom of Kalos' voice challenged the boy to continue humming and walking. For a moment he could not hear his own humming as the power of Kalos' voice thundered upon him. The boy looked deeply within himself to find the true source of his humming. The power of Kalos' distorted and empowered voice continued, but gradually the boy was not taken hold of by it and avoided being drawn into the maelstrom.

As the sounds continued to swarm, the boy continued his inner exploration. He was able to move on without the security of the old architect's hand. His whole attention was set on his humming. Eventually, it was so deep and wholesome that the boy lost all physical sensation. His arms and legs were gone. He could not tell if he was blinking, he could not feel the turn of his head or sound in his ears, he could not feel the cave floor beneath his feet. The absences of normal sensation did not bring panic, just a subtle curiosity in the unknown source of his humming.

Only this gave him a sense of identity. It was consistent and clear and he felt deeply calmed and assured in the seeking of what was within him.

Suddenly the boy was struck with the shuddering shock of his physical form's return. He fell to the ground as his physical self compelled him to not forget, to not relinquish his body. He slumped into a ball, crying and sweating. Myana, too, was struck with a similar experience.

The old architect's hands lay upon the boy and Myana, but they had no sense of him. It was all they could do to focus on accepting their bodies and to regain the comfort of their physical form. When the onset had lightened, they trembled with the oscillations rippling through their bodies. Their entire physical body was realigning. The boy heard a distant hum somewhere behind him. The maelstrom of Kalos' voice was now a soft drone. They had moved through and beyond it.

They stayed there for some time. None of them spoke, and with the return of the two children's physical form, sleep overcame them.

In their slumber, again the old architect left them in his cloak but returned before they awoke. The old architect roused them gently and helped them to their feet.

"We are almost through," he whispered, as he gave Myana the edge of his cloak and turned to lead them on. The boy held the collar of Myana's woollen dress and they resumed their journey. The smooth surface of the chamber soon became uneven again. Moving through the caves once more, the boy felt the depth and strangeness of his experiences recede like a dream.

Footsteps echoed through the dark of the encircling rock.

4.

A distinct dripping of water.

And then, in the dark they had journeyed through for so long, came the disruption of light. A single cell, the finest filament pointing through the dark, it hung in the air making the surrounding black, deeper. At first, the boy thought it was something in his mind, an illusion, but then the glimmer became haloed by jagged rock.

"Have we been walking up?" the boy asked in a dry, cracked, voice.

"Yes." There was subdued excitement in the old architect's voice.

"For how long?" the boy said.

"Since we last rested," the old architect said, and the boy could not remember when that was. "This is the last. It is an exit."

The boy stopped and looked up at the aperture in the rock; the light shimmering through softly. At regular intervals a distinct bright point would form at the top of the opening then disappear, followed by the sharp sound of a drop of water. The boy was surprised that it was still night; their journey seemed to have been much longer. Even though the opening lead out of the caves the soft glow was not a welcome end of rest and nourishment. It was a lighter dark that required more of them. Their whole journey underground was ending in a pointed dark that only bled a fragment of light one drop at a time.

"It is very steep and slippery," the old architect said, looking at the final rise to the exit.

"I want to sit," said Myana as her chin drooped.

"No." The old architect pushed passed the boy to reach her.

"I want to rest. I am tired." She slumped into the architect's hands.

"Do not sit," the old architect said with compassion.

The girl looked up towards the exit. "It is not far, but I cannot go up there. I am tired…and…I like it here." Myana's breath began to become very heavy. "It is calm, it is peaceful." With what little light fell upon her, the boy could see that Myana was smiling.

"If you sit, I cannot carry you. You have to walk alone."

"No," she spoke slower now, "I want to rest." The old architect supported her as she slumped to the cave floor.

"Please Myana, come with us," the old architect said. The boy heard genuine fear in his voice. Then the old architect leaned in close to Myana and whispered in her ear. The boy could not hear what he said. "No," Myana said gently. She spoke again and it was so delicate that the boy could not make out what she was saying, and then he understood. "It is alright." But when she spoke her voice was not as it had been. It was somehow deeper, it made her sound older. The boy could just make out the old architect looking at her with similar perplexity.

The old architect propped Myana against the cave wall, cradled her head and his expression became sad. Then he kissed her forehead.

"Why can we not rest here for a moment and then go?" the boy said, looking at Myana's obscured face. He tried to recall her features to complete what the absence of light could not.

"We have a momentum, a rhythm, lingering would be treacherous if we disregard it," the old architect said.

"But we have already lost Meneth and Kalos," the boy pleaded.

"I know. I said this place was different, it cannot be helped. We must go on. That is the only way out that I know of and we can only exit one at a time." The old architect's tone had become very calm and neutral.

"Why?"

"Because that is the nature of this exit and that is how things are here."

It was then that the boy realized how powerless the old architect had been in the caves. He had guided them, but he was as vulnerable as they were.

The boy looked at Myana and realized how tired he was. Seeing Myana in the soft light from the entrance, he envied her rest, the depth of peace within her. Her whole body was moving towards sleep. Her breath becoming heavier, the boy could see that with each inhalation she sank deeper into herself.

Watching her, the boy found himself becoming more and more aware of his own breath. The sounds of the cave were diminishing, his body was becoming heavier. With each breath he found more and more depth in his inhalations and exhalations, and so the spaces within himself became broader and more compelling. It seemed to him that the sound of his breath were echoing and reverberating within him, revealing other depths within.

"Listen!" the old architect's voice split through the boy's self-seduction of his own breath and splintered his mind into thoughts. The boy turned around quickly and the old architect moved to him. The little light that came through the exit illuminated the gentleness in the old architect's face. The old architect took a deep breath, very different than the ones Myana had been taking, and then spoke with an assertive calm.

"Listen." The sound of the old architect's voice drew the boy away from the enticing lull of Myana's breath. "You cannot hold my hand or my cloak. It is slippery here, and steep. Take each step with care, short and deliberate. Do not move until you can support the step you intend. You can brace yourself with the cave wall, but do not rely on it. Always look down. Be patient reaching the exit."

The old architect lead the way. He lifted his arms to prepare his ascent and the shaft of light was obscured.

"Follow me but do not match my step. Find your own." The old architect moved and his silhouette became fabric-like. The drape of his hair and the contour of his cloak rippled into one another. Ignoring the old architect's instructions, the boy watched his movements to find some guidance. As he watched, he held his breath in an attempt to make no sound, so that he may reach out and be as attentive as possible. He heard the shifting sounds of the old architect's steps and hands as he made his way up the passage. The old architect's movements were obscured by the drape of his cloak so the boy could see very little of how he was managing his ascent. Looking up towards the ambiguous silhouette of the old architect, the boy became gradually more and more aware of the drop of water that fell at regular intervals at the passageway's exit. The sound cut through all the sounds of the old architect's movements.

When the old architect was halfway up the passage, the boy began to follow him. The boy placed both arms on the cold rough cave wall. He placed one foot, lifting and then settling it on to the smooth passage floor. His foot slipped as though he had just stepped onto ice.

The old architect had already moved far ahead and was almost at the exit. The boy put his foot down again but the pressure made his foot slide. He tried again and found stability from his thigh. He tensed the muscle to hold his foot's position. To take a step he needed to enlist his back in a way he never had and the sensation of muscular strain creeped up into his spine. He stood there braced on the edge of the beginning of the inclined tunnel. He thought of Myana sleeping just behind him. He wondered if it was this effort that had compelled her to sleep. Did she know?

He heard the old architect ahead of him. "Find the momentum. Listen for it."

The boy had no idea of what the old architect spoke. He was on the verge of crying. It was too much to do, too much to ask of him. He had gone through so much already. Why this as well? The old architect was so far from him now he did not know where his steps had fallen. There was no guide, no direction, except for the the tunnel itself and what it demanded of him.

Braced within the passage, the boy recalled all he had gone through in the caves. He saw his family and imagined what had happened to them. His heart ached and his mind reached far beyond the passageway, to the kingdom, the destruction and the fire, the death and the malice.

"Listen." He heard the old architect's voice coming from outside the passageway. As he braced himself, the boy heard the droplet and remembered the shard of light it formed. Each time, the sound became a little bigger and the boy felt as though he could feel the impacts reaching him through the cave walls and reverberating into his body. As he listened more intently, he thought of how the light formed in each drop, and that it was only when the drop sounded that the light was gone. A euphoria came over him as he drew the image of the light forming in the droplet and the sound of its impact on the stone, into his body. They became a single element and all thoughts apart from the passageway dissipated.

His resolve started in his fingers, and as he dug in, the bone and flesh seemed to have no distinction. He pushed for leverage, but it was not a pure physical intention, it was a request for guidance, to be pulled forward. He compelled the droplets to move him, and that the stone of the cave be more than a challenge to overcome, he sought the volition of the tunnel. He exerted force into the cave walls to compel stone and water to pour into him.

As he reached out, he felt a return and took a step. Every portion of his body went into that single gesture. It was a soft movement, but it had flowed through him with a final jerk for his foot to reclaim a hold on the cave floor. From there, listening to the droplets, he saw and felt that concussion as a birth of light that would travel into him through the stone of the caves, and it motivated him. One after the other, slowly gaining understanding of what was required, he took a step and then repositioned his hands, but always with a slight force to summon the power to move again. He moved with pain and euphoria woven and oscillating throughout his body. He kept his head down and continued to align the droplets' sound with their luminescence. Every time he heard the drop strike the rock at the passageway's opening, a glimmer of light would ignite within him.

Soon he began to feel air from the exit wafting over him. Slowly the air revealed sounds of voices and activity. He tried to decipher them. "Retain your momentum," the old architect spoke from beyond the exit, beyond the droplet of light.

The reminder drew the boy's attention back to his link with the stone of the cave and the droplet of water. He saw the mountain in his mind and then he became the scale of the entire mountain. Now, every drop he heard not only passed light into him but through him to engulf the whole mountain.

Suddenly, he saw a roughness in the stone of the passageway floor where before it had been smooth, then grass beyond. The boy was completely immobilized by what he saw. One step up and he would be out of the tunnel. He braced his hands more firmly to prepare to make the step. He would need all of his remaining energy, wherever it was in him, to accomplish the simple movement. He thought of sliding back down, but would tumble down to its beginning if he did. He would be too weak to get up or try again. His mind flushed with the image of Myana's face obscured by her hair in the dim light; the depth and calm of her breath, her repose.

The boy took the deepest breath, which was now lush with the smell of trees. He stood braced against stone, feeling the strain and the support within his body and the entire mountain; a seal of profound connection. Then a droplet of water struck the crown of his head and he was propelled out of the experience. His hands slid from the rock face and the whole sensation of the mountain rushed out of his body. He dripped out of the tunnel's black.

He stumbled forward and beyond the cave opening. He fell to one side and steadied himself on a large stone then curled in on himself from fatigue.

It was night yet there was light of a distant, fiery glow and the air had ceased to be so cold and crisp. It smelled of smoke and coniferous fragrances, noxious and fresh. The boy let his grip slip from the stone and fell to the ground, where he lay face down in the grass and began to cry. A hand touched his back. Another hand on his shoulder. He was gently lifted.

Crying framed in surrounding arms, trees and destruction beyond.

5.

The banging of wood and a rapid unfolding of light.

The old architect had made a fire. For the boy, the light rekindled the memory of his in-and-out of consciousness as the old architect had carried him down the mountain. He had smelled smoke, heard voices shouting, "Over there, there!" Sometimes he shook and trembled in the old architect's arms as he ran. He had heard the old architect grumbling to himself, but it had been mostly incoherent. Only "It is alright, we are almost there," was clear.

Eventually the old architect had eased the boy to the ground with a light pressure on his shoulders and a gentle, soothing, "Sit," as the old architect tried to catch his breath. The boy sat crosslegged, slouching forward with fatigue as he heard fragments of the old architect busying himself. There was a faint background of distant violence.

"Where are we?" the boy asked.

"At the base of the mountains," the old architect said as he turned.

Now with firelight, the boy watched the old architect disappear into the surrounding dark as though he passed through a curtain. The ground was level and hard, peppered with grass. They were in a surround of trees, some of which were on the slope of the mountainside and looked spectral in the flickering light. I have never been beyond the mountains, he thought.

The kingdom was situated on a large plateau within the enclave of a ring of mountains. Children were never allowed to leave the kingdom, and the boy often wondered what was beyond. For him the horizon had always been mountains. Now he was on the other side of them, and he could see nothing but what the fire before him allowed.

When the old architect returned, it appeared to the boy as though he brought back a portion of the dark in his arms. Only until the old architect placed it near the fire could the boy recognize what he carried - a black stone. It had very jagged edges. The side facing the stone revealed veined lines and the boy remembered touching the steps in the caves.

"Do not concern yourself. They will not see this fire, their own fires have all their attention," the old architect said, and then departed again, soon returning with another stone. Each time he brought back a single black stone and placed it with great care, sometimes shifting previous stones to accommodate the new addition. The boy found the old architect's attention to detail, of interest, like he was placing the stones for more than the simple task of making a circle for a fire. It was as though the old architect was rebuilding the dark around the fire, piece by piece.

When the old architect placed the last stone, he sat, and together they looked into the fire. The boy wrapped his arms tightly around himself against the cool of the dark behind him.

The boy again noticed the veins in the black stones encircling the fire. More of the caves now came to mind, not only his journey down the steps but also the continual dark of the caverns. His reverie exploded with the image of the blazing boulder crashing through the window of the old architect's tower chamber and he was overwhelmed by images of the kingdom's destruction. Both events seemed unbelievable to him. He did not know which one was more acceptable - the attack or the journey through the caves. Anxiety and anger grew in him. He chose the one with less pain.

"How long were we in the caves?" asked the boy.

"Not very long, a few hours."

"I do not understand what has happened. I feel like we were in the caves for a long time, days, weeks." The boy bent towards the fire. "I do not understand. Why were we attacked? What happened in the caves? Where are Meneth, Kalos and Myana?"

"Not everyone responds…feels the same way when they are in a mountain. It is very different than being on it. And those caves…" There was a breaking sound from out of the dark. Both of them looked into the black. "Wait here, I will check." The old architect walked out into the dark and returned quickly.

"It is nothing," he said coldly, and sat again across from the boy. The old architect looked into the fire, and continued. "I first discovered those caves when I was examining the grounds. My predecessor, who had established and built much of the kingdom, had not completed the area where the tower is…was. When I surveyed the land I found an opening to the caves. I have spent some time down there alone. But not enough to truly know it. It is rich with passages and places and easy to get lost. The exit we used was the only one I had found. That was the first time I have travelled through it in complete darkness."

"How could you find the way?"

"I listened…" he smiled, "…and remembered."

"What did you remember?"

"The moments that I had been down there, in its dark." The old architect looked deep into the fire then added more branches to the fire from the pile he had gathered. The fire grew and the sound and heat soothed the boy.

"Fire was the first architecture," the old architect said.

"What?"

"Look into the fire and tell me what it is." He waited for the boy to respond. "Go ahead, look at it, what is it?"

The boy looked intently at the flames and watched how they moved, appearing and reappearing.

The old architect continued. "There are things you know about the fire. It burns, it is hot, it lets you see in the dark, you can cook with it, it can have different colours, smoke rises from it, it has a particular sound. But even with all that, you still cannot say exactly what it is. This is not because of what it is, but what it is a part of. This is why we do not understand what happened in the caves. This is why we all have incessant questions, because no thing exists out of its context, and so no question exists on its own. To answer your previous question, I do not know what has happened. For other people entering the caves it would have been different, just as being attacked was not our choosing."

"But people do not disappear."

"Yes, they do, because to say someone or something has disappeared means you cannot explain it. It is formed out of questions and questions are infinite. For every answer one receives, more questions arise." The old architect fell silent as he shifted the burning wood with a stick and flames rose up.

"This is Hax-Sus."

"Hax-Sus? What is Hax-Sus?"

"It is an old word…an old sound. Hax-Sus, in the simplest terms, means the desire to know. Hax-Sus is about why we sit here together now. It is about why Meneth, Kalos and Myana are not here. It is about why you came to see me this evening. It is about why our kingdom burns. It is about why the trees grow, the leaves rustle, why the sky is above us." The old architect fell silent with a gentle smile. The distant violence rose a little.

The boy felt a deep sadness overtake him. He began to think of his family and his mind found images he did not want to see. The old architect walked over to the boy, sat next to him, and put his arm around him. The boy leaned into him and felt the lush texture of the old architect's cloak drape over him and onto his wet cheek.

The boy watched the fire. The old architect's words were hard to grasp but somehow he felt an understanding. He was attracted to the ideas, he liked the words the old architect used. But he was tired and his mind did not want to continue those thoughts.

"What are we going to do now?" the boy said wiping, his cheek and looking at the old architect.

"I was just going to ask you what you are going to do now," said the old architect.

The question worried the boy. He thought maybe the old architect was going to abandon him.

"What I mean is, you get to choose. You may come with me or you may return to the remains of the kingdom. So there are two choices. That way," the old architect pointed up the mountainside towards the distant din of violence, "or that way," he pointed to the dark opposite the mountain. "Either back to the kingdom and what may come of encountering those who attacked us, or out into the dark." The old architect went silent as he looked into the fire.

"What is there?" the boy said.

"For me, Hax-Sus. I wish to seek, to understand, Hax-Sus." He was silent for a moment, the fire crackled. "Everything I have done, made, is gone. I want to know many things, and I am done with Kings." He looked at the boy and smiled. "I have many questions."

The boy looked into the fire. It used to be warmth and comfort in their farmhouse. Now, with the attack, fire was something else; it was not a simple thing anymore. He too had many questions. "I will go with you to find Hax-Sus."

"I am very pleased by your decision. Then we are going to seek Hax-Sus." The old architect looked back up the mountain where the smoke rose, where the din of activity continued, "Not the way they have. We cannot stay here too long, it is too dangerous."

They were silent for a moment. The sounds of distant violence hung in the air with the cracks from the fire.

"But first, we are going to do an ancient ceremony," the old architect said. "Not many people now know of it." He turned and sat facing the boy. "A long time ago, when people would meet and they felt a strong connection, they would choose a name for one another. They did this because it meant that they were saying 'I know you, and I want to know more about you.' This is what we will do now."

The old architect took the boy's hands in his own.

"Now, look into my eyes, and feel my hands in yours. Breathe deep, deep into your belly. There is only the two of us. See my eyes, feel my hands, and listen." The words trailed off into the fire. The boy felt a warmth fill his body and he tried to pick a name. Looking into the old architect's eyes he could see a depth that frightened him and yet the feel of the old architect's hands was so soothing and comfortable. The two sensations retained an opposition he could not reconcile.

A shiver went through the boy's body. "Listen." Again the old architect's word trailed off into the sounds of the fire. A profound calm came to the boy. It was brief, a flash, but as gentle as a blanket wrapped around him. In that calm, a sound rose up within them both, and simultaneously, they spoke each other's new name.

They held hands a little longer, gently coming out of the experience and the boy was no longer frightened by what he saw in the old architect's eyes. They smiled at one another. Then the old architect rose.

"Tomorrow we will begin our journey. For now, sleep. I will keep watch." The old architect placed more wood on the fire.

The roar and crackle illuminated the circle of black stones.

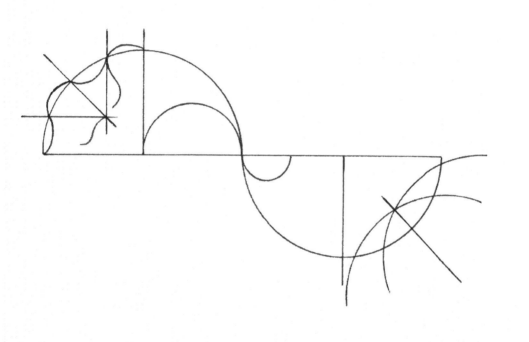

6.

A voice called for another.

"Taso?" A deep gentle voice in the unfamiliar dark.

Taso knew that it was for him, but exhaustion held him in the tight curl of sleep.

"Taso." Gentler still the voice spoke. He kept questioning the idea of himself, his thoughts softening and sharpening, back and forth.

When Taso opened his eyes, it was still dark but the very finest essence of light was colouring the black and giving line to the horizon against a background of grey. Then self-identity settled in as he recognised the hinting of dark blue that moved and changed depth. Then he knew it was him. He was Taso.

When his eyes cleared and he sat up, he was in a surround of trees at the base of the mountain. Looking up towards the mountainside, he could see rising black smoke through the leaves and branches. The smoke was of thin lines and plump accumulations breaking apart or swirling together. The whole process was slow and gentle. The air was so still and all the airborne debris of the night's carnage rose up as lumbering contemplations of the mountains.

"Gaum?" Taso's throat was dry.

"Yes."

"Where are we?" Each word Taso spoke softened and moistened his speech.

"On the edge of the plains." Gaum said as he stood facing the approaching light pouring into the dark of the grass landscape. "We must move." There was distance in his voice as he focused on the horizon.

"Where are we going?" Taso slowly came to his feet.

"First to find water, and then," Gaum paused and smiled, "Hax-Sus."

Taso looked out to the plains then moved drearily to Gaum's side. With the oncoming daylight, the plains opened like a book skyward. Taso looked back to the mountains and the billows of smoke that loomed over them. Then he looked at the remains of their fire. A ring of stones with black charred remains at its centre, gradually becoming clearer as the surrounding shadows receded.

Taso looked on to the plains once more. They watched the sun, Tor, rise.

Gaum turned to Taso, smiled and grabbed his wrists.

"Walk as upright as you can. And from now on when you walk, sit, sleep, at every moment, keep your palms facing in towards you. Like this." He turned Taso's wrists in towards his belly and made a slight cupping in his hands.

"Can I put them in my pockets?"

"No. It is the space between your hands that we are heightening. This will help you stay alert."

"For how long should I leave them like this?"

"Until you feel a change."

"I am thirsty." Taso finished his plea wiping the dry from his lips with his shoulder. Gaum gently repositioned Taso's hands.

"Keep your mouth closed for some time, breathe only through your nose, then swallow. That should help until we find water. Remember your hands."

"We could find water here, near the mountains. There must be water nearby."

"No. We could, but the source we need is out on the plains and it is not safe for us to linger here. It should not be far." There was excitement in Gaum's voice.

Taso felt the need to avoid harm, but he felt anxious venturing out onto the unknown of the plains. He could hear multitudes of people stirring on the other side of the mountain. It was distant but the emotional depth of it was close. He shivered. Gaum put his hand on Taso's shoulder.

"Let us begin," Gaum said, and began walking. Taso followed.

Taso had never been on the plains. His entire life had been within the kingdom. He had known so intimately the house where he had been born and the borders of the small area of land his family cultivated. His neighbours and the small groves in between the waterways and the paths about their area of the kingdom.

Taso had only visited the central castle for a few royal ceremonies and occasions. He knew there was more of the kingdom to see as he knew there was a world beyond the mountains encapsulating the kingdom. But he was a farmer's son and he was needed by his family. The kingdom had strict guidelines for all its citizens. Each citizen had their role and expected outcomes in accordance with the greater needs of the kingdom.

Taso did not enjoy farming so he took every opportunity he could to find new places or new things in the places he knew. At an early age, Taso's mother recognized his creative abilities. First, it was in what he told her of his dreams. He saw strange places and creatures. Later she began to find arrangements of stone or wood into tiny structures, shapes and figures drawn in the ground or on stone with charcoal. She asked Taso if he had made such things, he said yes, and added that he could not help himself. Sometimes he would carry images in his mind and they would not leave him until he had created them. Months later, on a rare visit to the grand courtyard of the central castle for the arrival of delegates from another kingdom, Taso's mother found him staring at a statue of the king with deep interest. She asked him if he wanted to be king. He said, "No, there is a mistake in the statue, the face is wrong."

Soon after, she had brought Taso a bound collection of paper. He then began drawing using fragments of charcoal.

His father was averse to Taso indulging in his interests, but Taso's mother quietly encouraged him. She had taken him to the base of the stairs of the tower. "You must go alone. I will wait for you," she had said.

When he could find time for himself, and if the weather permitted, he would draw outside under his favourite tree. It was an immense tree with deeply grooved bark and great branches that arched out into long draping leaves, forming a curtained sanctuary. It distanced Taso from where he was so that images could come into his mind with extreme clarity.

As Taso remembered sitting beneath the tree, he saw it catch fire. Why was she not there when I came down during the attack? He became anxious and listened to the soothing sounds of his steps in the grass.

With each step Taso watched Tor rise and a unique feeling of well-being presented itself to him. He could certainly imagine great expanses of open grass when he was tucked within the formed limits of the kingdom, but he did not suspect he would find it so inviting to be beyond the boundary of the kingdom. It felt right to be walking out on the plains, under a vast open sky. He wanted to run in release, but it felt improper. It would not be in accordance with the pace Gaum was setting, nor would it be respectful of the ordeal they had just experienced, fleeing the attack on the kingdom. I should not be happy, he thought.

Thoughts of the kingdom's ruins brought sadness and Taso's sense of comfort diminished. A great pain swelled within him and overtook the brief, expansive pleasure he was experiencing. The images of his family and the damage of the kingdom engulfed his mind and felt as though they would consume him. He thought again of running, this time to escape what he was feeling. But again, running did not seem appropriate. As his thoughts were unsettling and frustrating, he focused on a direct and stable reference - his hands. Peace of mind came as Taso ensured the correct orientation of his hands. Gaum had placed them so they were just below his navel, as though he were holding his stomach if it were much bigger.

Taso stopped walking to correct the position of his hands. Then he looked up, Gaum was quite far ahead of him and appeared as a sliver of black in the thick light that came from Tor. Taso walked on with a quicker pace but it was difficult to maintain the position of his hands without looking down. Eventually his pace slowed again.

Beyond Gaum, Taso could see only a gentle sloping land of shifting pigments offset by Tor's brilliant light. He stopped again to look more carefully at the horizon. Further on, the land appeared to level into distant ambiguous features. Their course looked as though it was a flat extension into light.

How long does it go on? he wondered as he moved his gaze back to his hands. To another kingdom? Between his cupped hands he could see his feet brushing and pressing the blades of grass. Will anyone follow us?

Question after question emerged from one and into another. They were seamlessly joined. He hesitated to ask Gaum these questions; they seemed far away, complex and clumsy. He feared he would disturb Gaum and the calm and comfort he felt of the plains around them.

Taso remembered what Gaum had said about Hax-Sus. "We all have an incessancy of questions, because no question exists on its own." Taso imagined the questions Gaum had.

As Taso walked he heard a faint sound. It was gentle and coming from within the sounds of grass beneath his feet. It was the flow of water; they had come to a stream. It coursed through the grass like a vein crossing their path.

Taso was so thirsty. He placed his hand in the water; it was so cold that it stung his hand and sent chills through his body. He cupped some water and brought it to his lips knowing that it would sting again. His lips and teeth felt brittle as he drank. His whole attention was on pushing through the discomfort of drinking as he forced the water into his mouth and swallowed.

Having drank some of his fill, he watched the ripples of water and the disruptions his hand and drops of water had made as he drank. He cupped the water from the stream again and looked up to see Gaum on the opposite side of the stream kneeling a few steps from him.

Gaum was bent over the water, and with both hands, he held what looked like a piece of animal skin over the surface. Taso continued to cup and drink water as he watched Gaum. Then the skin of the vellum began to bulge in the middle between Gaum's hands. Slowly it rounded up evenly at its sides and moved inward. The material rose up more and more within Gaum's hands, forming a mound as it rose up and away from the flow of water. It was hard to tell whether he encouraged or controlled the process. When the edges of material began to reach his hands, he moved his palms gently to the corners. He extended his fingers and thumbs to meet and somehow it all joined, and in his hand he held a sphere.

Taso rose and walked until he was opposite Gaum across the stream. "What is it?" Taso asked.

Gaum said nothing. His eyes were different and he handed the sphere to Taso across the stream. As Taso took the sphere, Gaum collapsed to the ground as though some great force had knocked him back.

Taso watched Gaum as he lay on his back and spoke skyward. "It is done, it is done, it is done." Taso moved to the edge of the stream, trying to catch Gaum's eyes as he continued repeating, "It is done."

Taso could hear a change in Gaum's voice. A breaking. The deep calming tones of his voice were loosening and something else in his words was appearing. Gaum spoke the words louder, almost to the point of shouting. Then he was silent and stood up.

Gaum looked into the stream, following its path with his eyes, then looked out to some distant place on the horizon. The air was still. Gaum turned to Taso. He found Taso's eyes and smiled with a genuine, warm affection, and then began to cry.

Gaum covered his face with his hands and sobbed and moaned. Taso could not tell if he were an old man or a young child. Taso was overwhelmed and helpless, and the sight of Gaum crying made Taso want to cry. But he stood there, holding the sphere as he watched Gaum.

The discomfort of the moment overtook Taso and he jumped the stream. He went to Gaum's side, unsure what to do. He watched Gaum sob into his hands. Taso wanted Gaum to stop. He wanted Gaum's voice back. He wanted Gaum's presence that had brought him through so much. Taso could not believe what he heard coming from Gaum. He could not believe it was the same voice, the same person.

Feeling he had no other option, Taso put his hand on Gaum's shoulder. Taso held it there as Gaum cried, and he seemed unaware of Taso's touch. It was some time before Gaum's sobbing lightened and he slowly brought his hands away from his face. Gaum looked around as though he were in a new place. Taso could see how exhausted he was. Taso kept his hand on Gaum's shoulder and sat down next to him. The stream flowed on before them.

Then Gaum spoke softly, "It is done."

"What is done?" Taso asked cautiously. Gaum pointed to the sphere of water Taso held. Taso looked closely at the sphere. There was an opening of water and its circumference was a smooth edge formed by the animal skin folding into the sphere. Taso tried to see deeper into the sphere but the water was dark. He moved the sphere a little and he could feel a slight pushing and pulling that compelled the opening of water to remain skyward. It wasn't very heavy but it felt more solid than he had expected it would.

Gaum took a deep breath and said, "When I was young, about your age, I saw this." Again he pointed to the sphere, "In fact, all of this." Gaum's hand gestured over the stream and then to the land beyond it.

"There were many times I tried to force the making of it, but I could not. It never happened. For years I have carried that skin and this." Gaum showed Taso a small bag; inside was a drinking flask. "They have been with me for so long. But I never thought it would come with..." Gaum choked back tears. "I never thought it would be realized after such devastation. The kingdom," he looked to the stream, "those children in the caves." He paused again and looked down at his hands. "I could not guide them through it."

"You guided me," Taso said. Gaum looked up at Taso, his old eyes so young now, innocent. The sight overwhelmed Taso and he looked down.

"You saw this, how?" Taso said, motioning the sphere to Gaum. Gaum reached for it and gently lifted it from Taso's palm.

"Yes, in an evolving dream, a vision really. I saw an old man make this."

Light reflected off the liquid opening of the sphere. "I was a boy watching an old man make this compass."

"It is a compass?"

"Yes, a very special one. It is a compass for Hax-Sus." Gaum paused and looked at it intently. "But that is all I know. Where it will take us, how it will take us, I do not know. In all the times I have discussed and explored Hax-Sus with others there has never been any mention of this." Gaum held up the spherical compass, turned it, admiring its shape and features. "This is the limit, the boundary of what I am aware of and I have no idea what it will bring." Gaum continued to gaze upon it and whispered, "An infinitude of questions."

Taso matched Gaum's tone and whispered, "Hax-Sus."

"Hax-Sus," Gaum repeated, sounding more assured. He looked at Taso. "I am glad you are here with me."

"As am I."

Gaum lead the way as he held the spherical compass. They did not speak as they moved further across the land. Tor had climbed towards its zenith as the air warmed. For the duration, Taso had shifted his focus between his hands, his feet and thoughts of the compass. When he could, he would look to see it in Gaum's hand. He alternated carrying it in both hands, always with the liquid opening pointed skyward.

Taso was becoming more accustomed to holding the position of his own hands without looking, while the sound of grass under his feet was of greater interest to him. The sensation of stepping and walking had become more physically invigorating. The sound of grass being moved and weighed down by his step was revealing more intricacies; there were moments when he thought he heard the distinct shift of each blade under his step.

When his thoughts wandered away from the sounds of grass and the positioning of his hands, Taso's mind would find questions. How was it possible for Gaum to make the compass? How will it show us the nature of Hax-Sus? Where will it take us? Taso's questions linked and rolled from one to the other, and then he remembered, "No question exists on its own." Does that mean that Hax-Sus is only questions? If so, then could we ever learn what Hax-Sus is? Maybe we will go nowhere?

All these thoughts were exciting, his mind and his heart opened to them. Yet he still carried anxieties and fears.

There was a quick churn of air about them. Further ahead, a distant wind rose. It left in the soft punctuation of a far off thunderclap and carried on in a decaying, gentle roar. Gaum and Taso stopped in unison when they heard the sound. Then the air became uncomfortably still for Taso. He felt the sound had heard his thoughts and forcibly stopped his questioning. Gaum held the compass with an outstretched arm and then leaned his head down slightly. Everything was so still. Taso felt vulnerable in the silence.

"Listen," Gaum said. Taso dare not move.

Gaum turned his head slightly towards Taso without looking at him. "Your palms are not facing in." Taso quickly looked at his hands and then corrected them.

"Rest. We need to rest." There was a perplexity and euphoria in Gaum's voice. Taso walked to Gaum's side. He looked tired.

"Are you alright?" Taso asked.

"Yes." Gaum shook himself a little. He looked at the compass. "I think it is making me tired."

Gaum pointed to an area of grass that seemed no different then any other place in the plains they had come across throughout the day. "We will rest here."

"How long?"

"Until we need to continue on."

Gaum went to his knees, whirled off his cloak and stretched out on it as he smoothed out the ripples and creases in the heavy fabric. Lying on his back, he held the compass to his belly with both hands. Taso went to the ground wondering how to take his cloak off.

"Do not forget your hands," Gaum said sleepily, his eyes already closed. Unable to determine how to remove his cloak and retain the position of his hands, Taso chose to leave his cloak on and rolled on to one side. Tor shone brightly. Taso was not accustomed to sleeping in daylight. He found it difficult to relax into sleep with so little notice. Taso looked at Gaum's hands; they were deeply lined and held the spherical compass as a ring of mountains.

Taso placed his hands upon his body in the same place as he had held them throughout the day. He thought of how he might turn in his sleep and rested his hands above the fold in his shirt. He closed his eyes and waited for sleep.

Taso's body rebelled with irritations: an itch, the hardness of the ground, a tautness in his shirt and cloak that pulled against his neck. He did as best he could to right the aggravations without moving his hands.

When the physical intrusions to sleep subsided, his thoughts went to the kingdom and his family. He tried to ignore the images and bring his mind into synchronicity with the plains' placidity. But he could not and so he opened his eyes to the sky and to Tor's brilliant burn.

Taso turned his head and looked to the distance they had crossed. The height and scope of the sky was intensified by the ephemeral grey of smoldering debris coming from the mountain range. The smoke had succumbed to the sky's expanse and become a thinning smudge as it ascended. In his mind, Taso could hear the sounds of their night's journey through the caves: the bursts and violent assaults of destruction that had come from above, the reverberations of their footsteps, their laboured breaths through the caverns, Myana's breath when they had slept under the cloak.

In the corner of Taso's eye, Tor retained a sharp tinting. With the aerial mark of the smoldering kingdom and the bright beacon of Tor, the blue in between felt as a vast emptiness bisecting heat and fumes. He lay there watching the smoke rise and Tor move towards it. The prolonged observation would make his eyes tear, and so he would close his eyes, cleanse his vision and repeatedly watch the slow trajectories of the smoke and Tor.

After some time, Taso had still not fallen asleep and then he heard Gaum moving. With his gaze still fixed on the horizon, Taso said, "I could not sleep. Tor is so bright."

"Hmm…" Gaum rose with new vigour.

Taso turned to see Gaum adjusting his cloak. Taso held back the questions that sharply returned to his mind the moment he heard Gaum waking. His questions were comprised of so many others, a great chain of empty links. His queries diminished as he rose with great care. The importance of the position of his hands took the focus away from his mind's doubts and demands, and when he stood he thought of Hax-Sus and found Gaum looking at the spherical compass.

"It is an interesting sensation." Gaum spoke as Taso walked to him. "It coincides with other experiences I have had. It is a kind of push and pull. However, no heat."

"Is that what you feel, heat?" Taso asked.

"It can be a part of it…sometimes the pushing and pulling becomes heat, and more…sometimes."

They looked at the spherical compass. The opening of water reflected a fragment of the sky.

"We tend to sleep to be active," Gaum said. "We do not consider activity for the purpose of sleep. And so, sleep is an obligation, not an invitation, nor something that is cultivated due to activity. This is one of the first questions about us, about being alive and about Hax-Sus: what is sleep and what is being awake? When I became tired, I think it was partially because of the push and pull, but also, there feels to be…an invitation."

"An invitation?" Taso asked.

"Yes, what I am following, it feels like I am being welcomed or called."

They continued across the plains. The sky had changed. A line of cloud stretching the entire length of the skyline was approaching. Taso turned and arched back a little to see Tor behind them. It had begun to descend. Where does Tor go at night? Does it burn like fire, does it need wood? Why is it round? Why does move across the sky the way it does? Does it move away or get smaller? Has Tor always been in the sky?

"Taso, your hands," Gaum said gently and turned as he lead them on.

The clouds moved steadily towards them in a uniform masking of the sky. Their colouring reminded Taso of the smoke rising above the ruins of the kingdom, but the clouds were never in separate clumps. They moved as a single mass obscuring the sky and casting a dark shadow upon the bright green of the land.

At times Taso felt shifts in his balance originating from subtle movements in between his hands. He stopped walking to focus on what he felt. He looked at them and saw nothing. Yet the sensations were perceptible. They were cloud-like movements of the space between his hands, soft and gentle. As he focused on the sensations, the shadow of the oncoming clouds draped over him suddenly. He turned and watched the shadow move over the grass. Looking up he saw the edge of cloud approach Tor. Its beams softened and the shimmer of its blinding light dwindled. For a moment it was a milky circle with soft pulsating edges, then the thickness of cloud blotted out much more of the light and it was a glowing silhouette.

The perimeter of shadow the clouds cast continued to the mountains and the fallen keep of the kingdom. When the shadow covered the mountains, it seemed to Taso that the world hushed to listen to itself.

Taso remembered his favourite tree. A great roar of fire and flames overtook him and the sight of the distant mountain peaks was a great pain. He began to feel and hear all that had transpired on the night of the attack.

He started to cry. His sobs sounded muffled by the shroud of grey clouds above. Everything around him began to retreat. He felt frustrated, powerless, insignificant and lost. He wanted to bite down on his teeth until they shattered.

Gaum put his hand on Taso's shoulder. He shuddered, surprised to find Gaum so close behind him when so much of the world seemed to be recoiling from him. Gaum put his arms around Taso and cupped his hands in his own. Taso leaned back a little into Gaum, his vision blurred with tears.

"I cannot stop thinking of my family, my mother, my sister, my father. They…." his voice collapsed.

"They…" Gaum whispered in a soothing tone.

"The sounds of their voices, their screams, they are moving closer and closer. They are in my body. They are filling me," Taso wailed and fell completely into Gaum's arms.

"A kingdom is an attempt at a great pooling of consciousness." Gaum said as he began stroking Taso's head. "People gather, find a place and try to sustain something beyond them, conducting, separating and synthesizing virtues. It began long ago and it will continue. It has its benefits and its drawbacks."

Through his sobbing, Taso heard and felt the depth and richness of Gaum's gentle voice as though it were behind glass. But as the voices and noises grew inside him, he heard less and less of Gaum's words and soon he could not hear his own sobbing. His mind and body were consumed with the husk of his father's voice, the silvery sweetness of his sister's words and the soothing tone of his mother's speech, all of them being exerted and tortured into sonorities of fear and pain. Within that melange of his family's cries and calls came a mixture of violent concussions; breaking and burning; stone, wood and metal forcibly deformed.

Gaum could feel how Taso was receding into himself. He turned Taso to face him. Taso saw the tears in Gaum's eyes, but the look on his face was not sadness, it was profound perception and action. He could see Gaum reaching out to him through his gaze but he could not feel it reaching him. Taso wanted to be what he saw in Gaum. He could hear nothing beyond himself; inside was an immense storm of twisting and distorted sounds that echoed and sang of pain, violence, and despair.

"Taso, focus on my voice. Find my voice." Gaum felt the anxiety growing in his own words, he paused and looked over Taso to the mountains. Dark smoke still rose from within the peaks. He took a deep breath and then fixed his gaze upon Taso's eyes and said, "Listen."

Taso felt Gaum's voice before him and he reached out to draw it in.

"Taso…Taso…" The tones and feeling of the sounds began to reach Taso a little. That name, that sound, its familiarity reached him, not only from outside of him, but from within as well.

"Listen. I know they are there within you, but listen within and without."

Taso felt great comfort from Gaum.

"Listen within…listen without."

Taso remembered crossing the large chamber when Kalos' voice filled the entire space. He felt now as he had in the chamber: overwhelmed with echoes and reverberations that had amplified and grown to such a degree that he was no longer audible within himself. He did as Gaum said - he listened.

Gradually he found the sound within that he had formed as he hummed in the cavern chamber. It was a minuscule clarity, a comforting luminescence that sounded through the din of destruction, pain and suffering.

"Listen." Gaum said again.

Taso's inner cacophony lightened a little. He wanted the sound to fill him completely. He tried to hum but it was not the same sound as his voice; all he could do was cry. He fell to the ground. Gaum held Taso as he cried. The release of his cries came more and more from the unknown source within him. He wanted to fill the plains with his own voice as Kalos had done in the chamber. He wanted everything to be his own voice, free of what he heard of his family inside him. But in the plains, even with the cloud cover, his voice did not carry as it would have in the caves, reverberating and filling the air around him. In the open air his voice went to unknown locations in unknown directions. It was carried so that he would never know how it would change, grow or diminish. His voice was another question.

Eventually, his cries diminished and he was exhausted by the release. They sat together for some time on the plains. The clouds blanketed the sky and muffled the landscape.

"Why do people kill? Why do we die?" Taso asked.

"Taso, I cannot explain why. I can give you reasons. I can talk about people's fears and their greed, their power-mongering. I can speak of how we are born with the vibrancy of living then grow old. I can speak of how the body has many systems and aspects that are extremely resilient or easily exposed and damaged. But really, at the core of everything, I do not know. I, like you, wish I did. I would love to know why, to have a degree of control that my imagination and my heart cry out for, but I do not have this."

Taso was calmer now, yet still saddened by what Gaum had said.

"And then I think about what I do have," Gaum continued, "and when I really go inside myself I am gladdened to find even more mystery, more unanswered questions."

"What do you mean?" Taso asked.

"You see, the questions you have, the uncertainties, the inability to feel a sense of closure or certainty, is not an absence, it's an invitation. Everything gets bigger, deeper. The kingdom is no longer a kingdom, you are no longer you. Because, as we move through life, what we consider to be us and what we consider to be outside of us, both are open and expansive. The questions roll on within us and around us. They too are expansive and deep, and so there is always more." Gaum's voice rose in excitement, "Yes there is pain, there are fears, but there is much more, and you will not know that if you do not listen, and listen in a particular way. When we only listen to what is within us, or only to those things outside of us, this is when in fact we are not listening. Listen within and without, bring them together. And you did, and you came through this experience."

They were quiet as the stillness of the cloud shadowed the plains. Then Gaum said, "Do you know how I became the architect of the kingdom?"

"No." Taso said with a slight crack in his voice.

"I was able to give the king the first thing he asked me for and it was the last thing I wanted to give him."

"What was it?"

"A weapon."

"Which weapon?"

"That is not important. What is important is that I can equally create what I believe in and what I do not believe in. All of the skill and knowledge that I have is based upon my capacity to choose. We do the same with our thoughts and our actions."

Taso looked at the mountains and then turned to see the opposing horizon. It was a complete contrast to the mountains, flat and featureless.

Gaum continued. "You feel sadness now, but there will be more. Anger, joy, bewilderment, clarity. You will carry the love you have for your family with you for your entire life, just as you will carry the pain of losing them. But there is always more. Because when you listen, truly listen, you acknowledge this time, this place you are in. With your whole-self you can delve into the richness of how they all intermix, how they are a unity."

Taso continued to focus on the horizon and took a deep breath. He moved to get up. Gaum put a hand on his shoulder and said, "There is no urgency." The air became still. "Take what time you need."

The words resonated deeply.

7.

Footsteps in the grass.

Taso listened for the silences between his steps as he and Gaum walked side by side. Gaum had encouraged Taso to move gently after being so overwhelmed by the images and thoughts of his family.

For the most part, their course had been a leveled progression of even ground and still air. The softening shroud of cloud that covered the totality of the sky cushioned the ruffling and stirring of grass beneath their feet. Eventually, Taso found the grass moving under his step comforting and it felt good to move again. They had not spoken for some time, and with his hands becoming more and more comfortable positioned out before his belly, Taso was able to be more aware of his stride and the open air of the plains.

Gaum stopped and held the spherical compass out in front of him.

"What are you doing?" Taso asked.

"I am feeling the direction of our course."

"What does it feel like?"

"Here." Gaum handed the compass to Taso. It felt very much like it had when Taso held it right after Gaum had made it, but now the movement of the pushes and pulls were also around his hand. There was no change in the movements when he held the sphere in his other hand.

"What is that? Why is it moving?"

"I do not know," Gaum said with a calm excitement.

"But you are using it to show us the way. Why would you do that if you do not know why or how it is moving?"

Gaum smiled and then gently took the compass from Taso's hand and said, "We do that every day, in every moment. We move continually with mysteries and certainties. This is another aspect to Hax-Sus. Like motion and stasis, we are always sure and unsure. Right now we know that we are on the plains but we do not know where we are going. We know that we are standing on grass and land but we do not know the size of the world - we want to know. We want answers to all our questions. We are in a continual state of certainty and mystery. Things we know, things we do not know, things we cannot know, and it is in that culmination that Trust appears. This is why Hax-Sus is so important, because in may ways it is about Trust."

Taso looked at the opening of water. Light reflected off the still surface.

"Why does it not spill out?" Taso asked.

Gaum smiled. "I do not know."

Taso touched the water in the opening. The water resisted as he tried to push his finger inward. He removed his finger and there was no moisture.

"Does the light or the water show you the way?" Taso asked.

"No. It is the push and pull, the invitation, that guides me."

Taso wondered what the compass would help them find and what they would learn of Hax-Sus. Then he remembered "*the incessancy of questions.*" If that is true then would they ever know what Hax-Sus is? Would this journey go on forever? The thought overwhelmed him. He wondered how it was possible for Gaum to have made the compass. It seemed impossible and he wondered if his own hands could make such a thing.

Looking at his hands, he pondered their potential and power. "How did you know how to make it?" Taso asked.

"As I said, it came to me in many dreams."

"So you saw yourself making it, or did something or someone in your dreams tell you?"

"It was a mixture. But really, it was not what I saw but what I felt. Without knowing how or why, I knew I could." Gaum looked up at the clouds. "We need to move again. I feel stopping is not appropriate."

"Is that what you feel from it?"

"Yes." Gaum did not sound completely sure. "Do you feel able to continue walking?"

"I am tired and hungry, but I think I can walk more."

"I am hungry as well. In the morning I will find food. It is pulling me towards that horizon," Gaum gestured the compass forward, "and it is getting dark."

Taso now noticed how dark it had become and looked down at his hands. He wondered if he would be able to maintain the position without looking.

"The dark on the plains is like that in the caves when the sky is clouded over." Gaum said. "It would be best if you stayed close to my cloak."

Taso felt the word *caves* resonate profoundly in him and he felt anxious. Taso looked up at Gaum. "How can I hold your cloak?" he asked and gestured with his arms.

Gaum laughed and draped the edge of his cloak over Taso's hands. "So that we can maintain the position of your hands I will walk slowly. We will move at a relaxed speed so you can keep my cloak over your hands. We will do it together."

"Why can I not hold it?"

"Because your hands are positioned towards you and holding the cloak will turn them away. Turning them inwards builds your awareness of them."

"What will I feel?"

"What is there."

They walked on at a very slow pace. Gaum's steps kept a steady rhythm. Taso could not take the same strides, but soon he found his own pace to match Gaum's speed, and so they moved with two different yet complimentary pulses. The sound of the grass beneath the respective rhythms of their steps intrigued and invigorated him.

After some time of being absorbed in the hypnotic charm of the rhythms they created, Taso shifted his attention to the section of Gaum's cloak over his hands. He looked carefully at the material. He admired its drape and the folds of the material. The latticework of the thread was hard to see clearly as they walked, but the last of the remaining light caught the fabric and gave it a light sheen. Taso continued to look at the cloak until it softened and then disappeared into the dark.

Taso could see nothing, and within the first moments of pure darkness he felt an anxiety he had experienced in the caves. He felt an impending threat that at any moment something out of the dark would grab him.

"How are you, Taso?" Gaum asked.

"Alright."

"Am I going too fast?"

"No."

Gaum walked on at a steady pace and his voice lessened Taso's anxiety. He felt greater comfort being with Gaum and he was able to recognize how the dark of the plains was unlike it had been in the caves. Within the reverberant hard dimensions of the caves, they were under a perpetual threat, confined within cave walls and trying to get out. But on the plains they were free to move about, seeking Hax-Sus and guided by the compass. There was no pressure and no feeling of doom; there was an unfolding and a mystery that Taso felt very comfortable with. In the caves he felt something would reach him or take him; on the plains he felt the opposite, it was he who could reach out. He began to feel giddy, similar to the joyful feeling he had felt earlier, and he wanted to run.

As they walked on, Taso felt a shift in the sensation of the cloak draped over his hands. The physical feeling of the garment gradually retreated until it had disappeared all together, as did the sensation of his hands. Where they met was now a blurred and amorphous warmth.

Taso looked down at his hands and could see only darkness, but what he felt was a warmth becoming a tingling sensation. It intensified until it was a pulsation that spawned a luminescence. Taso could not see it with his eyes as he saw daylight. He felt the luminescence form and emit from the region of his hands.

The sensation continued for some time until it moved beyond the perimeter of his hands and extended into his entire body. And much like his experience of humming in the caves in the maelstrom of Kalos' echoes, he could not find the exact source of the light he felt. He spent the night walking through the dark with the curious light.

Listening to radiance.

8.

The rhythm of grass and breath.

At daybreak, Taso could see the clouds above them. They looked like an inverted landscape of white sloping hills that he looked down upon from a solid plane of black.

Seeing the quick pace of the clouds moving across the sky, Taso's footsteps felt as though they gained more distance than they ever had and he was invigorated by the dawn. The luminescence within him had been his focus throughout the night, but now he left it and let himself enjoy the thrill of stepping and moving over great distances in the oncoming brilliance of Tor's light. Taso's stride was not only of a forward motion but it was fuller and had an expansionary effect. In every step, Taso felt a radiance extending beyond his feet throughout the land of the plains around him. He gently let the cloak fall free from his hands and he came to Gaum's side.

"Tor is rising." Gaum spoke with fatigue in his voice after a long silence through the night. The words made Taso tired and he felt a deep weight in his legs.

"When will we stop walking?" Taso said.

"Very soon," Gaum replied.

Taso felt a relief that came with a weight filling his body. He thought of his hands and the light he had experienced during the night. He looked down hoping to see a lingering filament but there was nothing. A cold sensation came to him there and he ensured the correct position of his hands.

Taso looked up and and saw blue sky at the distant perimeter of the passing clouds. The air was very still even though the clouds gently drifted overhead. The movement perplexed Taso. Am I moving forward? Are the clouds moving towards me or is the sky pushing the clouds? His fatigue deepened. He was transfixed by the shifting elements of the world around him and felt a stirring depth, thick and powerful. He stopped walking, he was speechless and breathing heavily.

Gaum said nothing as he moved to the ground and lay on his back. As before, it was an elegant movement. He spread his cloak on the grass, turned, and then laid on his back holding the spherical compass to his belly. Taso followed and found a spot close to Gaum.

"Rest well," Gaum said.

Taso closed his eyes. The land felt as a cradle. He watched the last of the great blanketing length of cloud pass over in the diminishing fissure of his closing eyelids.

Later, when Taso awoke, he found Gaum sitting up on his cloak.

"Come sit with me, Taso."

Taso sat on Gaum's cloak. Laid out upon the cloak was a small sack and a waterskin. The sack was full. Taso looked bewildered.

"I brought the sack and the waterskin with me, remember?" Gaum said. Taso recalled the moment Gaum had shown him at the stream. The memory of Gaum crying was uncomfortable and he let the memory go. Gaum opened the sack and removed some root vegetables.

"Where did you find them?"

"Out on the plains. Not much grows out here besides grass, some flowers and these roots. They are delicious. They grow near streams, so I filled the waterskin as well."

Gaum handed the waterskin to Taso. He drank quickly at first, and when his initial thirst subsided, he drank slower and with greater care.

When Taso had finished drinking, he handed the waterskin to Gaum who motioned to the roots and said, "Choose three. Eat one now, then the others throughout the day. Eat another whenever you are hungry. For now, these should be enough until we find more to eat."

"How do I know which one I should eat first?"

"You know." Gaum paused, offering Taso to find the insight for himself. "It is the one...."

"...I need!" Taso blurted out.

"Yes!" Gaum was pleased by Taso's response.

Taso looked over the roots. Gaum had cleaned them, their skins were damp and light brown. They were of varying sizes and subtly contorted as roots commonly become as they grow. Taso chose a medium-sized root and brought it to his mouth. He knew to bite deep and chew slow. He thought he must savour it. He bit into it and then looked at the flesh inside, it was a light purple. Taso had never seen a vegetable like this before. He turned to Gaum with an expression of surprise.

Gaum said, "You never know what colour they will be, some are orange, yellow, even a mixture of colours."

They ate in silence for some time, then Taso said, "I want to talk about our walk in the dark last night."

"Very well," Gaum said through bites as the spherical compass lay on his cloak, its liquid opening catching the light.

"Last night my hands really changed, and I felt light in between them and in my body. It was warm."

Gaum smiled. "What I have showed you is an old method of exploring sensation in your body."

Gaum watched how Taso was eating. "Is it not interesting how only now you are really realizing how hungry you are. When we shift our focus it is possible to feel and notice other things, and so what usually occupies our minds and sensations retreats or does not become so important." Gaum continued to eat.

"But why would I feel light like that? How can I feel light? And why did my hands feel soft and not like they usually do?"

"I believe this is a part of Hax-Sus, about movement and inactivity. Asking me why is there fire, or why do the stars appear in the sky would be asking the same question, which leads to…"

"… more questions," Taso said.

"Yes."

"You have felt this as well?"

"Oh, yes. All through my body and from other people."

"Really?"

"Yes, give me your hands." Gaum put out his hand and Taso held it. The moment their hands touched Taso could feel a warm surging sensation coming from Gaum's hands.

"How do you do that?" Taso asked.

"The same as you, I can feel you doing it as well."

"You can?"

Gaum let go of Taso's hand and said "Yes, you are not aware of it and so you are not able to manipulate it. But you will." Taso pondered Gaum's words as they ate in the silence. He examined the shifting pigment of purple as he ate the root.

"Questions are for your whole self. They are not only thoughts in your head. Your whole body questions. So questions are about experience."

Gaum held up the remains of the root he had been eating. "Imagine you try a new food, or you smell a new flower, or see something you have never seen before, a new experience is about questions. Before, during and after, it is full of incessant questions and that is Hax-Sus."

Taso pondered what Gaum had said, then asked, "Where does the idea of Hax-Sus come from?"

"It is a very old idea, as is the sound of its name. Where exactly, I do not know, but it is an idea that I have heard about all my life." Gaum looked out on the plains and the spherical compass. "The word Hax-Sus is actually two words, Hax meaning motion, and Sus meaning no motion. But the deeper meaning of these two words is that Hax means change, and Sus means stasis. They are spoken together because they are one and the same. They cannot be separated and yet we experience them as two different things that are always shifting. Because they are inseparable, people believed they are the centre of everything. No matter how you see or touch or sense in any way, everything is fundamentally of that centre. For this reason, it is believed by some that Hax-Sus is the ultimate measurement of everything. If you understand Hax-Sus you understand all motion, all stasis, and so you know everything."

Gaum watched Taso finish eating and said, "Think for a moment about how hungry you were. You have fed yourself. Then you will not feel hungry as your body will change the food you ate without you thinking about it. You do not have to sit here and focus all your attention on the food going through your body. How certain are you of what is going on in your body? Why are there things we can do without thinking about them? Why does the body do it on its own?"

"I do not know," Taso said.

"This is what I meant about the experience of questions. It is our whole selves, our bodies, our minds and our feelings. The vibrancy of being alive is itself full of questions. Do you remember being born?" Gaum said with a smirk.

"No," said Taso. The question surprised him; he had never really thought about it.

"There are some who wish to have this knowledge and this control of questions, so they start with their bodies. They practice certain techniques so they not only know more about their bodies but also how they feel and what they sense. Some also practice to have control so that they know and they can be free of the questions. The impulse for an answer is about measurement which is knowing how something is in relationship to something else."

"Do you do these practices?" Taso said.

"Very few of them. I learned for awhile from different masters, but there are very few techniques that I have continued. Most of them are not my way. I do not believe in many of the practices."

"Why?"

"Some of them were dangerous or required absolute isolation. I enjoy people's company from time to time." Gaum smiled mischievously at Taso.

"Is what I have been doing with my hands one of those practices?" Taso said as he looked at his hands.

"Yes."

Taso looked up to the sky. He remembered looking into the dark of the tower's conical roof and wanting to know how to build it. He remembered trying to see into the dark, now he wanted to see into the sky and know its construction.

"Do you believe we will find Hax-Sus?" Taso asked.

Gaum pondered the question and then smiled, saying, "I do not know. But what I do know is that it is the root question of my life. Besides, it may find us."

"What?"

"When I explain Hax-Sus, I am telling you things that I have heard, things that I have experienced, things I believe. For me there is another part of Hax-Sus that is very important. And this, I think you have experienced for yourself in the caves and when I made the compass. It is a feeling and a knowing, an understanding and a desire." Gaum looked at the compass and picked it up. He looked out to the horizon. "The old beliefs say that because we experience things changing and not changing there is no reason not to suppose that it is the same for everything. All things have a knowing of change and no change. The grass, the sky, the animals, your clothes, all the threads that make it whole, they all experience change and no change." Gaum gestured to the half-eaten root in Taso's hand. "Even while you eat, the whole root, every bite, every part of it, all have a way of knowing that things are changing or not changing. That is how they are what they are. This is how they keep their shape and colour. And so Hax-Sus is in everything, it is a part of everything, and for that reason, everything is questioning, everything is seeking an end to questioning by its own knowing."

Taso looked at the bites he had taken of the root.

"But honestly, Taso," Gaum smiled as he spoke, "I do not know what Hax-Sus is but I want to know." He put a hand on Taso's shoulder. "You have felt a change in your hands, so if you like, you can hold them as you want now."

Taso looked down at his hands; he wanted to see into them. He smiled and said, "I feel like I have no idea what they are or what they can do."

"Exactly," Gaum said, as he ate some more.

The sharp and wet crack of a root.

9.

The smooth rubbing of hands and footsteps in the grass.

Taso was fascinated by how similar they sounded. He had been rubbing his hands as he continued to wonder what they were capable of. He had allowed his arms to sway freely, oscillating like two pendulums with varying synchronization. At times he would swing them together, back and forth feeling the weight and motion of his hands. They felt the same but were no longer the same to him.

The horizon before them had retained an even and undisturbed line. But now, points and jagged elements began to appear. Taso thought they might be trees, "A forest?" he said, as he pointed to the horizon.

"Yes," Gaum replied, deep in thought.

They stopped simultaneously. Gaum focused on the compass then turned to Taso and said, "At this time, it is guiding us to the forest." They walked on.

Having kept his hands fixed at his belly for as long as he had, brought new and invigorating experiences. Now that they were free to move about, he was conscious of them in ways he never had been. He wondered what was happening when he used and moved his hands and what effect that had on the things he touched and held. The luminescence he had experienced brought so many more questions. What was that light? What would happen when I drew? Was there a light then? Is the light always there or only at certain times?

Taso looked up at Tor; the light was strong and made his eyes tear. He looked away. What is the light that I felt, is it the same as Tor? The first similarity is that they were both warm. Feeling the light between his hands and looking directly at Tor both had their limits. They do not last forever. Tor comes and goes, does the light I felt come and go as well? When?

Taso looked down at the grass as the burn of Tor's light left his vision. As his sight cleared, Taso focused on Gaum's shadow moving over the grass. The edges of the shadow were percolating and shifting quickly. The depth of one blade of grass to another formed so much movement on the perimeter of Gaum's shadow that it animated the figure beyond the details of his garments, his facial features or the depth of his eyes. The edge of the shadow was alive in such a way that it seemed Gaum was occupying and even exploring the grass through his shadow. It was like another aspect of him, or perhaps it was another life rich with experiences. And just as the shadow could not reveal the details of Gaum's clothes or face, neither could the shadow's experiences reveal their own unique depths. Perhaps there are too many or they are too fast. Observing Gaum's shadow brought more questions. Does the light I felt between my hands cast any shadow of its own? If it was a light that I felt, would it bring shadows into the world? If so, would those shadows be like the ones I see now? Maybe they would be different because the light I felt was different?

Taso picked up his pace until he was again walking by Gaum's side, comforted and energized by his presence as they walked together in silence.

"Walking makes me think so deeply," Gaum said, looking down at the grass.

"I, as well," Taso said.

"What have you been thinking about?"

"Tor," Taso responded excitedly.

"Hmmm, Tor." Gaum looked skyward for a moment and then smiled out to the horizon.

"What is it? What is Tor?" Taso looked up at Tor and then looked away quickly. Gaum looked up at Tor, shading his eyes as he moved his gaze to the horizon.

"Another old question." Gaum smiled.

"There are so many questions."

"Yes." Gaum smiled.

"Why does it help me to see the world, but when I look at it, its light burns my eyes? And where does it go after it crosses the sky? Why is there only one like it? And why, even though it rises everyday, are some days are colder than others?"

"And what of stars," Gaum said, "why do we see them? Why are there are so many of them? Why is it not warm at night as it is during the day when Tor is in the sky?"

"Yes!" Taso skipped a little with his reply.

"It is amazing. So many questions, each one as interesting and profound as any other. Sometimes they seem to be all one question, and at other times, each question seems completely isolated and does not connect with the others."

Again Gaum looked up at Tor, shaded his eyes and looked away. "Fire is the first architecture," he said.

"You said that at the mountain," Taso said.

"Yes, think of your home in the kingdom. What was at its centre?"

"The firepit."

"Exactly. Fire is the focus. It determines all the other conditions because it changes the air and the space. It not only needs the right conditions to be made, but it needs to be cared for. It may not shelter you, like trees or a roof, but it becomes the height of the endeavour to shelter yourself and to bring warmth to your body. It does more than change the space around you, it goes inside you. When you cook food or drink tea, it moves into the architecture of your body."

"The architecture of my body? But my body is not a building."

"Of course it is! It is assembled, not with stones or wood, but it is a coming together to have a form and function. Everything that humans build is based on the architecture of our bodies, the size of an entrance, the designs of halls and rooms."

"So, the body is the first architecture."

"No, because when we die we become cold, we fall apart. Our body decays and returns to the architecture of the world. It is the fire, it is the light inside us that holds us together. It gives us life."

"Is that like Tor? Is Tor fire, or is fire Tor? What about the light I felt the other night?"

Gaum laughed. "I do not know, those are great questions. Light and fire are peculiar. I do not know how they are the same or how they are different. But it is when I look at fire that I think the most about Hax-Sus."

"Hax-Sus," Taso whispered. He began to feel a sinking feeling in his chest. He was overwhelmed with the scope of the questions. He thought again about the light between his hands as he looked at them.

Gaum noticed Taso looking at his hands and said, "Is it not amazing how little we know of what we do and the effect we have on the world, on others. And yet Tor releases so much with no concern for where its light will reach and how that light will be received. It continually radiates."

In his mind, Taso saw his family and the kingdom burning. "Yes," he said.

Gaum heard a shift in the sound of Taso's voice. "When I am walking," Gaum said, "I like to spread my fingers and feel my palms stretching open. This brings more air into me, makes my eyes see just a little more."

Taso thought about his hands and tried what Gaum suggested. As he stretched open his palms he felt a lift, first through his hands and arms, and then through his back as it lengthened upwards. He felt taller. He breathed more deeply and the painful images and sounds retreated.

Gaum looked out to the horizon and said, "Every blade of grass that we step on is significant. And yet, we keep moving and walking without being able to take in each one with our complete attention. Our breaths, our heartbeat, everything we see with our eyes and what we do with our hands all suggest more if we could only be fully aware of it all."

After a few steps Taso whispered, "Hax-Sus." Again he stretched out his palms and then he attempted to stretch out sensation as Gaum had described. He reached out to feel every blade of grass, to become more aware of every breath, to feel every heartbeat as he broadened his sight. These sensations became richer and nuanced. They began to move beyond their boundaries and meet as they never had. Taso's stride widened. What was within him and what was outside of him came closer; then he saw his sister burning. This sight of her came so fast and it struck him deeply. Her hair was on fire, her skin crisping and draping off her. His sister, who had always put her hand on his shoulder, encouraged him, told him that she loved him, was burning up.

Taso fell to the ground. The image of his sister morphed into his mother standing over her burning daughter. She spoke but no words came and rocks fell out of her mouth one after another. Then he saw his father trying to put out his fields that were on fire. He used his rake but it too was burning. Every time he drew it back over his head, the teeth of the rake would explode outwards and send fiery debris on to even more crops. All around his father was fire but he did not burn, he just cried. Taso had never seen his father cry. The images and the emotions all churned and massed as one. Then they cracked open. "Listen!" Gaum roared.

Taso saw in Gaum's eyes a mixture of concern and focused intent. Gaum had called to Taso several times before he was able to reach him. Taso felt the moisture of tears on his face and his entire body was wet with perspiration. Being drawn out of his experience so abruptly stunned him. He stared at Gaum and saw his eyes soften to a genuine and profound look of care for Taso. He wailed and hid his face in Gaum's chest.

Gaum rocked him back and forth as he rubbed his back. Gaum repeated, "Listen, listen, listen." The repetition of the word and the rocking motion soothed Taso. The fires he saw diminished and he calmed down. He smelled the air of the plains and felt the texture of Gaum's cloak.

Taso pulled away from Gaum and looked at him. Gaum handed the spherical compass to Taso. The liquid opening righted itself to point towards the sky. It felt different. It had changed. Before, the push and pull was from deep inside the spherical compass and just beyond his hand; now the movements were much more focused to an area two or three arm distances away from the compass. Taso stood and held it up to the horizon. The movements reminded him of guiding his family's horse with its harness. When he would walk in front of the horse without looking at it, there were moments when the tension of the leather strap would slacken. He could feel the horse through the strap but not directly or immediately feel its movements in the same way as when the strap was taut. It was a feeling of connectivity over distance, moving together but apart.

Gaum stood up and went to Taso's side. "We come out of this world into a sense of being," Gaum said, "and then we insist on expanding that being further out and further within. We seem to wish for dimensions beyond what is immediately revealed to us, and so we question again and again. We want to identify the initial moment of the fire of life within us, the spark that made us. We want to know more about that which allowed us to be. We desire the knowing of that spark. There are beliefs that say all was made of an initial force, a voice, a thought or some movement. Something shifting out of or within, nothing. Are we not the same?" Gaum paused, and looked at Taso. "It can be very perplexing, knowing simultaneously that you are the spark and the place of its illumination." Gaum was silent and looked again to the horizon.

Taso felt the movements within the spherical compass. He looked at Gaum. It appeared to Taso that Gaum had just gone through as much as he had and that Gaum was far away and deep within himself. Taso held the compass up to Gaum. Sunlight reflected off of the liquid aperture. Gaum smiled and gently took the spherical compass from Taso's hand and said, "Rest a bit."

Taso smiled, "I want to keep going. The compass compels me to keep moving."

"I understand," Gaum smiled, "but give yourself some time. We will continue." Taso sat and passed his hand over the blades of grass.

The light staccato of grass accompanied the quiet of the plains.

10.

Wind whistled through the grass.

The land had remained flat and even all day. As dusk approached, Tor descended upon the mountains that Gaum and Taso had left two days ago.

In the diminishing daylight, Taso became more and more intrigued with the growing reach of his shadow. Its parameters became pointed and he found the perimeter of his silhouette fascinating. As it passed over the grass, he watched the varieties of depth between the edge of his shadow and the grass. He felt he was scanning very accurately their relationship and soon he believed he could feel his shadow brushing over the grass. As each blade went from being in Tor's light into the realm of his shadow, he felt the crossing and the transition.

Taso's stomach growled. He reached into his pocket and took out one of the two roots he had selected from the roots Gaum had found for them. He looked at its brown skin. The shape was much straighter than the other he had selected. He imagined which colour would be inside. The other had been purple and Gaum had said there could be all kinds of colours. Why are they different colours but the outside is always the same? Taso bit into the root and it tasted very much like the other, but it was a little sweeter. Inside, it was yellow-red. He ate more of the root and saw rings of bright yellow and deep red that seemed to glow.

As he ate, Taso once again watched his shadow. It had lengthened greatly in the diminishing light. He felt refreshed and nourished as he ate but his pace slowed and his focus on his shadow waned. He remembered Gaum's words on the uncertainty of knowing what happens in his own body. He tried to feel what he had consumed and he attempted to sense its journey within him. But apart from the soothing calm of a full belly, he felt nothing new as he finished eating the root. He returned his attention to his shadow upon the grass.

"Stop," Gaum said, as he abruptly raised his hand. The movement startled Taso and he jumped back. Gaum's hand shook a little from the intensity of how he spread it open. Taso froze, looking at his motionless shadow.

"Look." Gaum spoke softer now. There was a huge crater. Its edge a precise curve in which the land formed a uniform dip like a great bowl. It was so perfectly shaped that Taso wondered if it was natural or man-made. It was at least the size of one of his father's fields and it sunk down to about three times his height, or so he imagined. The grass of the plains lined its edges. With the oncoming night and the deep shadow cast into the crater, it was difficult to tell what was at its centre.

"We will rest here," Gaum said with a commanding tone as he sat a few steps away from the crater's edge. Taso joined him. "This place is different," he said as he moved the compass in the air, "and important." He sounded unsure to Taso.

"Was it made by people?" Taso asked.

"I do not think so, but something important happened here," Gaum said, deep in thought.

Taso laid on his belly and rested his chin on his hands. Gaum looked back, squinting at the last rays of light seeping from behind the mountain range. Then he lay back, bringing the compass to his belly. Taso watched the far edge of the crater disappear into the oncoming dark of night. They fell asleep quickly into their respective inner journeys.

When Taso awoke, the night was bright with starlight. He turned on to his back and looked up at the stars. He was in awe of the cosmic luminous stillness. He had seen the stars many times, but always from within the perimeter of the kingdom. Out on the plains the sky was far grander and deeper. Taso felt a gentle pull from it as though he could be lifted up among the stars and darkness.

Gaum was awake and looking into the crater. Taso turned on to his belly and looked into the crater. In starlight the contours of the crater were softer and more inviting but he was still unable to discern what was at its centre. Taso's curiosity was peeked and he was eager to go inside.

"This place is special," Taso said and turned to Gaum, "is it not?"

"Yes, it is." Gaum smiled and sat up. "We will cross it. The spherical compass has brought us here and the direction feels clear to me. We must pass through it."

Gaum stood, held out the compass and waited. He stood there for a moment with an inquisitive and playful expression. He looked like a child trying to decide what to do with a toy. Taso rose and watched Gaum walk to the very edge of the crater. Again, Gaum stood there waiting. Then he quickly knelt and placed the compass upon the edge of the crater with its liquid aperture facing upwards. He stepped back looking intently at the compass. Taso walked to Gaum's side, his eyes fixed on the compass. The air was very still. The compass rested motionless in front of them, and then with neither a sound nor any perceptible external force, the spherical compass began to spin, moving clockwise along the crater's edge.

They watched closely as the compass soundlessly spun and slid over the grass. As it continued to move away from them, it became smaller and smaller until it was a shadow. Taso squinted to keep it in his sights, but then it was consumed by the distance and surrounding dark.

Taso looked frantically for the compass all along the far edge of the crater but he could not see it. He stopped himself from asking Gaum where it was as he felt guilt for loosing track of it.

"Do you see it? I cannot," Gaum said.

"No, I do not," Taso replied.

They continued to scan the crater's edge. The anxiety Taso felt made him look in every part of the crater. For a moment he looked down in front of him, waiting, hoping to see the compass. He was on the point of suggesting they look for it when a short, bright flicker of light flashed at the far side of the crater. Then there was another and then another.

"Do you think that is it?" Taso said.

"Yes." Gaum sounded far away in thought.

The pulsating light grew into a chaotic and spastic flicker on the opposite side of the crater. The luminous display followed the smooth curve of the crater's perimeter, and then as it began to continue in the arc towards them, its reflections dimmed and then stopped.

Taso maintained the pace set by the distant light and estimated the position of the compass along the edge of the crater. Soon he saw it again but it was behind the position he anticipated. As it approached them he never let it leave his sight.

"How do you feel?" Gaum said softly.

"Relieved."

"Hmmm, I too am relieved." Gaum took a deep breath. "But I feel we need to cross the crater letting the compass continue around the edge."

"How do you know?"

"I do not know, but it feels right to do so."

The compass passed quietly in front of them without any change in its spin or movement across the grass at the crater's edge.

They walked to the place where Gaum had originally placed the compass. Taso felt that before them was an opening or a passageway. It was peculiar because it seemed to him that he was being invited into the crater. Taso watched the spherical compass bathed in starlight move away from them. He was uncomfortable letting it move along the edge as they crossed the crater, and yet there was this fascinating invitation before them.

Gaum stepped over the edge first and Taso followed. He felt a delicate shaking sensation that moved around and through him. It was brief but it assured him that being within the crater was not like the rest of the plains.

The slope of the crater required that they lean back to control their descent. In having to do so, Taso wanted to be mindful of where the compass was but needed to focus on his balance. Being drawn towards the crater's centre intensified Taso's anxiety; he remembered Gaum's words, "Hax-Sus is so important, because it is about Trust."

"I can feel the compass, can you?" Gaum said excitedly.

"Is that what happened when we stepped in?"

"I think so. What I have felt from the compass is all around me, us."

Taso slowed his step and focused more deeply on his balance. He became aware of another factor affecting his ability to walk down the edge of the crater. It was not only the grade of the land, it was in the air around him and within him. It was akin to what he had felt from the compass before. It was similar to his recollection of leading a horse, the strap being slack and taut, like a presence out beyond him aligning and re-aligning itself with him. This sensation was intensifying as he recognized more similar connections around him as they moved closer to the crater's centre.

Taso stopped walking and recalled what Gaum had showed him to do with his hands. He brought all his focus to his hands; he felt heat and tingling sensations within his fingers and weight in his palms. He moved is hands so they were close to the base of his belly and then he closed his eyes. Gradually he felt the turbulence of the multitude of pushes and pulls receding out beyond him so that the activity no longer passed within him. He felt his balance return and he continued in this manner further into the crater.

The grass thinned and the familiar sound of his feet moving through the blades diminished as he neared the centre of the crater. The ground underfoot was hard. The sound of his steps gradually changed from a smooth long swish to a crunch until there was neither a smooth contour to his steps nor a rough texture. It was now hard and flat. The centre was solid stone.

Beneath Taso was a black surface. He bent over and touched it. It felt smooth like the stone steps in his descent in the caves. He recalled the maelstrom of Kalos' reverberantly mutated voice.

Taso looked up at the stars. He felt an accuracy and an order to them that he had never been aware of before and could not voice. His feet rooted into the hard stone beneath him. Looking to the stars above he began to see stars beneath him. It was not sight from his eyes, it was an image that came from somewhere at the back of his mind. And although he knew he stood upon a very hard stone, he began to feel it rapidly thinning until it was transparent. At that moment the ground beneath him and his peculiar sight of stars beneath him came together. His hands dropped away from his belly and the multitude of pushes and pulls that were above and around him rose up from below and met within him.

Their unity held him and he was overcome with a profound realization. Their whole journey beneath the kingdom and within the mountain was folded. Like a piece of paper's edges may be aligned again and again, every moment in the dark of the surrounding stone, every sound and action, every sensation and emotion was a profound whole. So that all the dimensions were reduced but nothing was omitted. With the thought, Taso slipped into a lament for Meneth, Kalos and Myana. It was brief but it ceased the experience of the unity he felt within himself between the stars. The ground beneath him was again an impenetrable thickness, the stars above held their mysterious order, and the way the pushing and pulling had escorted him into the crater returned. Taso felt he was losing his balance once more and repositioned his hands at his belly.

Gaum had already begun to make his way up the other side of the crater. Taso followed and felt a peculiar resistance that seemed to be the crater wanting him to stay. It was not so much physical but emotional, as a soft and distant plea. He walked on hearing the hard stone of the crater's centre become the gentle brushing of grass.

Coming out of the crater Taso grabbed at the grass to assist in his ascent. The textures in his hands brought him back to his physical body. Leaving the crater, as when he had entered, he felt a vibrating motion pass through him and the surrounding air. He laid on his belly with his feet just beyond the edge of the crater, his breath heavy from the crossing. Gaum was on the ground and seemed pleased with the experience. Resting on his side, his arm propping his head, he looked back to the crater.

Taso's panting subsided; he turned on to his back and looked up at the stars. His experience at the crater's centre was retreating. The physical sensation of the grass and ground beneath him outweighed the memory.

"What just happened?" Taso asked.

"I do not know," Gaum replied contentedly. The compass passed Taso.

"Reach for it," Gaum said casually.

Taso stretched out on all fours. When his hand came close to the compass, the sensations from within the crater emerged between his hand

and the compass. It yielded to his grip and ceased rotating as he easily removed it from the crater's edge. Taso looked at the liquid aperture; there was a soft hue of starlight that appeared in the subtle movements of its liquid surface. The movements from within the compass matched what he had felt from within the crater.

"You keep it with you tonight," Gaum said with the sound of slumber in his voice and he laid on his back.

Taso laid back in the grass holding the compass with both hands at his belly. His fatigue deepened. The sensations from within the compass and beyond his hands softened. For a brief moment, as he was falling asleep, Taso remembered the sounds of his steps when he reached the base of the crater.

Shifting grass, rocky steps and a luminous silence.

11.

A spacious silence.

Taso opened his eyes to blue sky. He felt the spherical compass in his hands. The calming sensations from within and around the compass were now more active. There was a developing pull above Taso's head.

Knowing he had a direction given was comforting and so Taso took the time to bask in his view of the sky. There were no clouds and so it was a complete vista, nourishing to his eyes in its infinite impenetrability. He moved his fingers over the compass, feeling its smooth texture and allowing his thoughts to wander to their evening crossing of the crater. He remembered the compass travelling the edge. In his mind he saw himself in his supine position orbiting the crater as the compass had. Floating at the edge of its perimeter. Why would I see this or think of this? What happened last night? Was that Hax-Sus at the centre of the crater? Why did I see stars under me?

Gaum peered over Taso and entered into the rich openness of the blue sky that filled Taso's sight. "How did you rest?" Gaum said, looking refreshed.

"Well." Taso slowly rose.

They looked at the crater. In the morning light Taso could see how the grass extended into the crater and at its centre was a black stone surface. They turned to see the land that now gently descended into another open area of the plains bordered by a forest. Taso felt as though he had not seen a tree for so long and these particular woods looked odd to him. Taso turned to Gaum and said, "A forest, should we go there?"

"Perhaps we may walk a few steps and the compass will change its guidance. What do you feel from it?" Gaum asked.

Taso paused. Gaum's question confused him. *Is he asking me how I feel or which way the spherical compass is guiding me?*

His first inclination was to ask Gaum what he meant but he stopped himself. He looked down at the spherical compass, the sky reflected off of the liquid opening. He felt the smooth push and pull movements emanating beyond the compass. It was directing him to the forest. *How can I know the direction in this way? Why does the spherical compass do this?* None of his questions had answers, yet, he was certain of the direction to take.

"It is guiding me to the forest." Taso said. Gaum smiled at him.

Taso took the lead and they made their way down the slope of the plains. It was as deep a grade as the edge of the crater had been. The slope went far beyond them in both directions as though it were a much greater crater they were entering. Feeling the compass' guidance, Taso recognized how the descent was not as it had been in the crater with the multiplicity of pushes and pulls. Taso's stomach growled. With his free hand he reached into his pocket to eat the last of the three root vegetables Gaum had given him. He bit into the firm flesh. It was white inside.

As Taso walked on, Gaum slowly followed, giving him distance to avoid distracting him while he used the compass. Gaum allowed his mind to wander in thought as he watched Taso guide them. Gaum felt unease at the growing distance between them. He recalled their journey through the caves. His heart ached. He had been holding at bay the memory of the departure of the three children. *What else could I call it? I told Taso that they had disappeared but there was more to it. They departed. Not only death, but they left. Was it death?*

When Gaum first saw the children, he knew they were not like other people. He could not say why, but he felt that the caves for these children would be something very different than it would be for him and Taso.

Choosing to leave them in his cloak was all he could do to care for them while he ensured their course. It sickened him to have to leave them in that way but he could not conceive of any other way for him to guide them safely. Leaving and returning was so difficult as he never knew what he would find out in the caves or upon his return to the children. It was a harsh choice to make being their guide in the unknown.

As often as he had explored the caves, Gaum never did fully understand them. He had come close to perishing in their depths on a number of occasions. But he always went back because he felt he had gained some knowledge or understanding. The clarity of the importance regarding the spherical compass had deepened over the years of his exploration of the caves. Even though the compass was as much a mystery to him in its attributes as were the caves, it was a guide and that meant it was worth carrying its mystery to benefit from its support.

His heart ached when the boys had departed, but when Myana was at her threshold, he could not let her go without pleading, "Please, Myana, come with us."

"No," she had said, "I am where I need to go, it is alright." But it was not only her that spoke, there were more in her voice as though she spoke with others. And there was an age to her voice, she sounded older. *Or maybe that was the sound of the departure? But how, where? Is it a where? I am where I need to go? The oddity of the moment did nothing to* lighten the sadness Gaum carried for being unable to guide all of the children through the caves.

"Enough of this," he whispered, and pushed back the feelings and the memories. He focused on the sound of the grass under his feet and the forest before him.

Taso walked on, guided towards the forest as he ate the root. Gaum saw Taso eating and it made him hungry. He took out his last root and ate it. Taso and Gaum steadily walked down the gradually sloping hill of the plains as they drew closer to the forest. Gaum knew they would find more to eat in the woods; he was hungry but it was Taso he was thinking of nourishing.

When they reached the bottom of the rise Gaum was walking beside Taso. Without words or a glance, Taso handed the spherical compass to Gaum. Then Taso slowed his pace and Gaum moved forward.

Letting go of the compass brought Taso away from the singular sensory needs of its guidance and returned him to the prominence of his sight. He looked excitedly at the forest as they approached it. He wondered what they would find inside. He saw a gap in the trunks of the trees and a curving stone path away from the opening. Gaum was walking towards it.

Taso assumed that they would take the path and he began to think of the sound of walking upon it. He lamented leaving the plains; he would miss the open air and the sound of the grass under his feet. He imagined more of what would be in the forest. Darker images and possibilities surfaced and the sight of the trees made him nervous.

Taso watched his feet in the grass as he listened to the sound of the rustling blades. The sound was soothing and he remembered the quiet boat rides with his father upon the pond near their farm. He would watch the tip of the boat moving through the water. The movement of the two in his vision made him question whether the boat moved through the water or if the boat was stationary and that water moved against the boat. He wondered at the very same relationship of his feet walking across the grass.

Taso kept his head down as the memory passed and heard the sound of Gaum's footfalls on the rocky path. He matched Gaum's pace so that what he saw and what he heard were of two different experiences: his feet in the grass sounded like stones. Then the stone path was before him.

He stopped at the sight of it. He examined the edge of the path; the crushed rocks started very clearly forming a distinct grey line that contrasted with the green grass. Taso stood there as he heard Gaum's steps moving away from him along the stone path. He turned to see the rise of the plains they had just descended. The mountains were not visible. Taso looked down at the path and then took a step forward. The sensation was shocking. It was not as gentle and soothing as the sound and feel of walking on the grass. He continued along the path and with each step Taso's lament of leaving the plains became a growing anxiety for entering the forest.

Gaum had already walked to the edge of the forest. He stood on the path looking up at the trees. Taso walked cautiously towards him. The sound of stone under his feet retained the unease it brought Taso as he watched the height of the treeline grow and loom before him.

When Taso reached Gaum, he found him staring off to one side of the path. Taso looked in the same direction; there was a small structure. They walked towards it.

As they approached the structure, Taso could see it was a small narrow wooden house on a raised base of stone. Inside was a many-limbed stone figure. Standing in front of it, Taso saw how the face of the stone figure was split, one side angry and the other side joyous. The two sides met seamlessly through the mouth and through the features around the eyes leading to the bridge of its nose.

At the feet of the stone figure was a small empty bowl.

"What is it?" Taso asked.

"It is a shrine."

"A shrine? What is it for?"

"For prayer."

"What is the little bowl for?"

"For leaving offerings of food. You have never seen this before, have you?" Gaum said as he turned to Taso.

"No." Taso shook his head.

"It is an attempt to bring together thought and place. It is like a doorway."

"To where?"

"Purity. It is really the seeking of purity. To offset panic, find calm and to diminish questions."

Taso leaned in close to the figure to see the detail in its face. "Why does it look angry and happy?"

"Could you make one side of your face angry and the other happy?"

Taso moved his mouth and eyes to imitate the face of the stone figure. "No, I cannot." Taso chuckled.

Gaum laughed. "Look closely again, are both sides of the face really all that different?"

Taso looked again at the figure. What Gaum said suddenly made Taso realize that upon closer examination, both sides of the face concealed the other. The joy and the anger contained some quality of the other.

"I cannot tell which is which now. Which one is angry and which is happy? I feel they are both."

"Does it matter? If the two are not next to another but within one another, then we are both. That is why I said it is here for people to find purity. It is a desire to be free of questions."

"Hax-Sus," Taso said.

"Yes. For most this would be enough, but not for me. That is why I believe the dream of the spherical compass came to me. It is why you draw, even though you are a farmer's son, and even though, arguably, growing food seems to be a greater necessity than drawing, for you it is not."

"Why do you want to know Hax-Sus?"

Gaum huffed. "Because I gave the king a weapon and yet I also made this." He held up the compass. Taso continued to examine the stone figure. The more he observed it the more his original assumption of what he saw in its face dissipated.

"Why is the god small? If it is a god should it not be big?"

Gaum laughed. "That is a good point. But a point of focus can be of any scale, big or small."

They both fell silent and looked at the shrine. Then Taso looked to the woods and felt anxious about walking among the trees. Gaum noticed the expression on Taso's face. "What is it?"

"I do not want to go into the woods," Taso said.

"Why not?"

"I am not sure. Seeing this shrine outside of the forest makes me wonder what is inside. I feel that when we go in we cannot come out, or we will not come out because of what is in there. But I want to know what is in there. I want to go in and I do not."

"Sit, Taso." Gaum motioned Taso to sit in front of the shrine. Gaum looked at the shrine and said, "When you realize you need to build something you have a scale in mind because of its function. This is due to questions. Whether it is a home, a castle, a bridge or a farm, they are all responses to questions. Scale is then a moment of an answer. But new concerns will appear beyond the original intention. You need to consider other people, the ones who would attack or want to take what you have built. And so new needs and intentions become important, more questions, and so the scale changes." Gaum looked at the statue and placed his hand on its head. "And nature, too. It works against what you build. Weeds may grow through the floor you have laid; the wind blows leaves into courtyards; buildings need to be positioned for light; weather and storms erode the roofs and the walls; flooding, snow. Nature moves everywhere, a continuity of new concerns, more questions. I was taught to build according to nature. And yet whatever we build, regardless of its scale, it does not move with nature and nature does not support it. So, I do not understand scale anymore."

"Hax-Sus," Taso whispered.

"Yes. I understand why you are conflicted and why you do not feel comfortable entering the woods. But scale is Hax-Sus because it is about questions. When we are overcome with questions and we do as fear compels, we not only lose the potential for measurement but also our capacity to understand scale. This cuts us off from so much more, from experiences, insights and growth. I do not know what the more is, but I want to know." Gaum looked back into the woods, then turned to Taso, "So, I am happy to go in there with you." Gaum reached out his hand to Taso. He smiled and said, "Let us go together."

Taso took Gaum's hand. As they walked along the treeline, Gaum held the compass out before them. When they returned to the stone path, Gaum let go of Taso's hand and took the lead. Taso felt the sound of stones echo through his whole body. He had walked on many stone paths before but this time it was different. Entering the forest, Taso considered his apprehension and his giddiness. He wondered how the two were so often together as they deepened their journey beneath the forest canopy.

The clustered crunch of small rocks.

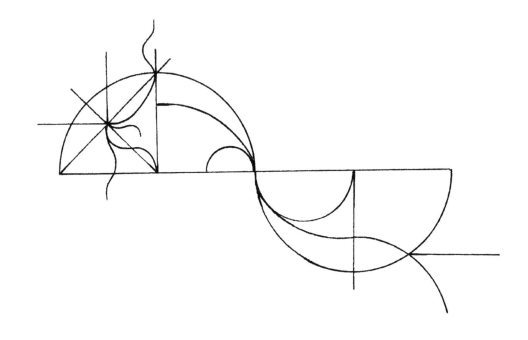

12.

Trees echoed stone.

Gaum and Taso's footfalls reverberated throughout the trees around them. Unlike the plains, the sounds of their journey audibly touched the place they were in.

Moving deeper into the woods, Taso focused upwards to the canopy of the forest. The stone path beneath him was what he heard and felt as his gaze was fixed upon the intermeshed branches above him. His initial feelings of foreboding continued as he marvelled at the surrounding trees. After their few days out on the plains he found the aromas and colours of the forest refreshing. He continued to walk on at a slow pace noting how the branches and leaves came together. His upward gaze and fascination were sustained until it all came to an abrupt end as Taso walked right into Gaum.

Gaum smiled at Taso as he held the spherical compass outstretched towards one side of the path. Taso looked to the woods beyond the direction of Gaum's hand and saw what appeared to be a new forest. The trees and even the light were dramatically different.

"We need to go in this direction," Gaum said as he looked down at the spherical compass.

They stepped onto the forest floor. It was soft and yielded deeply to their step, very unlike the hard base of the stone path.

Each step was a thick thump. Taso felt very different as he moved. The sight of the path had given direction while the sound and feeling of the path asserted a direction through him. The stone path was a very rigid way of moving and being moved. Yet, walking on the natural forest floor his steps sunk into the ground and he felt directions from within him moving out into the forest. Either course was uncomfortable for him. One was made for you, the other was made by you; in either regard you did not know where you would find yourself.

In this area of the forest the trees had grown spaciously apart, and so there was a freedom of movement dramatically offset by the brambles and bushes that had lined the path. Without the path, Taso mindfully stayed close to Gaum. Gaum remained fixed on sensing the compass' guidance. He was very calm and quiet. Daylight began to seep away and with the diminishing light, Taso's anxieties grew. He began to feel very much as he had in the caves. There was a similar vulnerability. Taso stayed close by Gaum's elbow as they moved on through the woods. Taso became more and more focused on the sounds he was hearing. Cracks and movements, some high above, others low to the ground. The deeper they moved into the woods the more he listened. On the stone path he had looked up, but on the natural forest floor he looked everywhere, listening more and more with his whole-self.

Gaum stopped and stood motionless as he had at the curve in the path. This time he looked ahead and whispered, "Look."

Taso could see the corner of a small house.

"Stay close. I do not know who we will encounter here," Gaum whispered.

They approached the house slowly. Taso followed Gaum and felt exposed to what may be behind him. When they were close to the house they hid behind a tree. The house was old and appeared to be in decay. It seemed no one had been there for some time. The roof had holes in it; the entrance was open.

Gaum whispered, "I will check the house alone. You stay here and hold the compass." Gaum put it in Taso's hand and then cautiously moved towards the house. Taso could feel the guidance from the compass leading towards the house as a fatigue began to set into his body. He wanted to stop walking and rest.

Taso watched Gaum approach the house. He was remarkably quiet and agile. He came to the house from behind and looked in the entrance way. Then he stepped inside. The entrance swallowed Gaum as he stepped through. Taso gasped as he saw him disappear into the house. It was fearfully still. No sound or movement came from the house, and then as suddenly as he had disappeared, Gaum emerged from the entrance. He appeared relaxed and he waved for Taso to come to the house. Taso was overjoyed to see him and ran to Gaum. The compass felt like a great weight with the deepening fatigue it fostered in him.

Taso looked around the house and saw a nearby firepit. Beyond it was an embankment and he could hear the gentle babbling of a stream.

"Taso, hand me the compass and look for wood so we can make a fire." Gaum reached out for the spherical compass.

"We are staying here?"

"Yes, for the night. I am going to look for food."

Taso handed the compass to Gaum. Immediately Taso's fatigue lifted. As Gaum held the compass Taso could see a fatigue creep into his body and his eyes. Taso went to look for wood.

In the time it took Taso to gather an ample amount of wood, Gaum had returned with a number of roots and a few varieties of mushrooms. He had also found some cooking utensils, a pot, a ladle and two bowls neatly tucked away in the abandoned house.

By nightfall they had made a fire in the firepit and the aromas from the pot were wafting through the air. Gaum served soup to Taso, filled his own bowl, and then sat. The spherical compass was poised on a stone next to him. They focused on their soup and did not speak, the cracks of the fire intermittently accompanied by the sounds of their sipping. Taso watched the firelight illuminate the trees around them.

Something caught Gaum's attention. He reached into the ground and pulled out a nail. It was rusted, twisted and bent. He looked at it and then placed it on one of the stones that encircled the firepit. "The nail was the end of the spiritual structure," he said, and then took another sip of his soup.

"When I was young," he continued, "I travelled to learn about architecture. I was fortunate to study with masters who build without nails. They follow the grain of the wood. In fact, they believe that in other lives, hundreds, maybe thousands of seasons before, they themselves planted the seeds that become the trees they work with. They look for these trees, harvest them and carve them into their intended function and shape. Their way is to interlock wood without nails. It is the wood that shows them how it joins." He smiled to himself. "There are few who do it now and fewer who can live with it. You must build a certain way without the use of nails. It decides a great deal of what you can build and what we build changes us. I learned a lot from them."

Gaum and Taso looked at the nail as they ate. The fire cracked.

"Every sound of a nail being driven is a blistering opening of the air," Gaum said. "The sound is inharmonious. It is a false rhythm, a discordant sound. It compels workers to chatter. It pulls them out of the work and out of the grain of the wood. It draws them away from the tree's life and its forest of origin. The clamour of hammering and distracted minds coasts through the air and changes the landscape. It is as war, like the pounding of steel on steel, forcing one rhythm against another."

Taso remembered the burning black stone in the centre of the chamber at the top of the tower and the spin of descending its staircase. He took the last sip of his soup and then rubbed his hands together.

Gaum cleared his throat and said, "Caves are a special architecture. People went to them first. There are those who still live in caves, hermits, madmen and mystics. They are seeking different paths but they do it in the caves of the world. Caves are the world sculpting itself. They are like the grains of the wood. I do not know what the world sculpted in those caves beneath the kingdom. They are different."

Taso recalled Myana's dimly lit face, the maelstrom of sound that had become Kalos' voice and the warmth of being under the cloak at the stream in the caves.

"When I first went into those caves," Gaum said, "I nearly perished. I went back several times. They changed Hax-Sus for me. They helped me accept what I had experienced in my sleep of the spherical compass." Gaum finished the last of his soup. Taso looked at the compass on the stone.

"How did the caves do that?"

"They made me question what I thought I already knew and so there must be more to know. The compass came to me untarnished by the opinions of others. Over the years I came to understand this uniqueness would offer new insights."

Taso could feel the dark of the caves, his fear, the vulnerability. The flickering of firelight on the house was in his peripheral vision. He felt there was life in the abandoned house as he looked directly at it. Every shift in the light reaching it seemed to animate an unknown life within and that at any moment some person, creature or monster would come through the door.

"What is it?" Gaum asked, placing more wood on the fire.

"The house, it frightens me."

"It frightens you?" Gaum asked pointing to the house.

"Yes."

"Why?"

"I feel as though someone or something will come out, and..." Taso stopped himself and looked into the fire. He wanted to hide his eyes, cover himself.

"Often the things we make need our continual attention, our care or else this is what becomes of them." Gaum gestured to the house. "Focus on the fire." He smiled and warmed his hands to the flames.

"Fire is the first architecture," Taso said gently within the delicate rumblings of the fire.

"Yes." Gaum echoed Taso's tone.

"Will we sleep in there?" Taso pointed to the house.

"No, it is not a good idea. The air is dank and unhealthy inside. We are better off sleeping outside."

"Who lived here?"

"I do not know, but it looks like they were trying to stay." Gaum looked back at the house then turned to the fire and said softly, "A tiny kingdom."

Taso was surprised to hear an edge in Gaum's voice he had never noticed before. He looked around at the trees illuminated by the firelight. Up beyond the leaves and branches was no sign of starlight.

"I don't know if I want to sleep outside either," Taso said, smiling anxiously at Gaum.

"We can make space anywhere at anytime. You remember how I would leave you my cloak in the caves?"

"Yes."

"That was for you to have shelter, to create a new space. Just as we are doing now with the fire."

Taso looked into the fire and then again to the trees above them. "I miss my tree."

"Your tree?"

"Yes, it was where I would go to draw."

"Ah yes, your charcoal drawings."

"How did you know?" Taso asked, surprised.

Gaum hesitated then said, "Your mother brought them to me."

Memories of Taso's family flooded his mind and his heart began to ache. He looked again to the house. He remembered eating around the firepit with his family. He thought of his mother's smile, his sister's long hair and his father's laugh. He saw himself with them around the firepit and then its flames spilled out upon them. They were draped in fire. The image made him shiver.

"Stay with the fire, Taso, and make a space with it." Gaum placed another piece of wood on the fire."A space of your own choosing."

Taso watched the ungraspable movements of the flames. He focused on the light and the heat to draw them in and push back the dark of the surrounding phantasmic trees and the house built of their carcasses.

"I do not like it here," Taso said as he wrapped his arms tightly around himself.

Gaum reached for the compass and then stood up, blocking Taso's sight of the house. He stood for a moment holding the spherical compass with both hands. Taso saw a fatigue weighing throughout his body.

Gaum looked at Taso with soft eyes and said, "We can make space anywhere at anytime. As fire is the first architecture, it is made in the right conditions and needs special attention. It is the same for the house," Gaum gestured to the decaying dwelling, "as it is for ourselves."

The fire cracked, reverberating through the trees and into the dark beyond the firelight.

13.

Branches creaked high above.

Taso kept his eyes closed as he listened to the dialogue between the trees, their branches receiving and responding throughout the canopy network. Opening his eyes he saw the firepit. He expected to see rising smoke but there were only dormant coals. Beyond was the abandoned house.

Gaum was nowhere to be seen. Taso rose, looked around and then went down to the stream. Still no sign of Gaum. He returned to the firepit. Where is he? Where would he go?

Taso looked at the house. He waited for any sign of movement from within it. He did not know why but calling out did not feel right. He doubted that Gaum was inside but he needed to check.

Taso went to the house. The trees cracked high above and he lightened his steps as he approached the house. At the doorway he placed his hands on the door frame, bent his head forward slightly and listened. He took a deep breath. Taso could smell the dank Gaum had spoken of the night before. It was heavy and thick. Taso looked back to the firepit and then stepped inside the house.

The wood floor creaked. Taso kept one hand on the doorframe. Inside there was a small table and chair in the centre of the house, a single window opposite the doorway, a bed to his right against the wall and to his left, a fireplace. There was little else inside except for the swirling colours and depths of decay; mosses and blackened unnameable areas that fed into deeply shadowed corners. Holes in the roof let in soft light and the movements of the trees.

Taso moved deeper into the small house and touched nothing. The floorboards creaked while the cracking of branches trickled in from the holes in the roof. He moved about to ensure there was nothing to fear. He inspected the dark corners.

The creaking within the house was as vivid and alive as the sounds of the trees moving high above in the canopy. But it felt as a living death. If there were a fire and people living there, that creaking of floor boards would be an activity of a different form of life.

Last night in his mind it was full of life; dark life that was waiting inside, silent and invisible. That at any moment something was going to burst out of the doorway. A different form of life so unusual he could not look upon without dying. Taso remembered Gaum's words, "We can make space anywhere at anytime. As fire is the first architecture, it is made in the right conditions and needs to be cared for." The house was ripe with an absence of daily life maintaining it; no warm chatter and preparation of food filling its dimensions to sustain life.

Taso left the house. He backed out of its entrance and continued until he could see the house among the trees. He remembered last night, how he had felt the dark of the woods and the house were alive and malevolent. That there was life in the dark, whether it was among the trees or within the house made of wood.

These thoughts had never come to him out in the dark of the plains. Again he remembered Gaum's words, "We can make space anywhere at anytime." The first night on the plains Taso had felt light, and on the second he had felt great stars all around him. "Fire is the first architecture." Gaum's words continued to come to him and Taso did not know what to make of these thoughts. He felt that they held answers but they seemed to lead him nowhere. "Hax-Sus," he whispered.

Where did Gaum go? Recalling his original intention, Taso walked beyond the house and in the direction the compass was indicating the day before. There were more trees. Taso touched them as he passed. From tree to tree, he felt the bark. Each touch was a unique pattern, a segment of a larger form that was full of paths and rough edges of more depth and more details.

Taso found Gaum sitting in a large stump in a clearing of other tree stumps. The light came down sharply on him. He looked like he was sitting on a throne, his head down and his arms laying in his lap. His heart and mind appeared heavy as though he had received some terrible news.

Taso walked towards Gaum, coming into the light of the clearing. The stumps held scatterings of new growth of small stems with delicate leaves and tufts of moss.

The stump Gaum sat in had been hollowed out by decay unlike all the other stumps which had been cut cleanly and had level tops. Its hollowed-out features made it appear older and nobler. Between Gaum's feet were a number of young plants, a minuscule world of green leafed stems.

"Another tiny kingdom," Gaum said morosely. "What do you suppose is underneath?"

Taso hesitated; he desired Gaum's mood that had brought them through so much. "Roots?"

"Yes and no." Gaum said as he grabbed some of the stems with both hands. He gently pulled them up exposing their roots and the surrounding soil.

"Look at that complexity," Gaum whispered. The intricate network of white roots woven into the deep dark soil harboured insects and tiny worms that scattered with the disruption. Taso smelled the ground.

"They are where they need to go." Gaum's voice broke a little. Taso heard pain.

Gaum breathed in and closed his eyes. "To know the means and reasons for directions, to have the experience of the movements, why this shape or that, what is being felt, all of it. What is this?" Gaum held the stems a little higher and Taso heard the roots pull and tear a little. "Yes, these are roots." Gaum looked up at Taso and whispered, "But where are they?" Gaum looked around his wood throne and he smiled. "Here in the soil. Within the shell of a dying tree that lives for them and with them. It is of them. Roots are not the root, they are only the boundary that we recognize between life and death, change and stasis. Where you see a root you find the remains of another root. Roots lead to more roots. Just like questions, they are infinite."

"Hax-Sus," Taso whispered.

"Yes," Gaum whispered in reply. "What is a king, Taso?"

The sudden change in topic bewildered Taso. "A king is a leader," he whispered.

Gaum leaned forward and Taso heard the soil beneath his feet give as a breeze moved the trees. Taso heard the depth of Gaum's inhalation as he began to speak. "That is what we are meant to believe, but a king is not a leader. A king is a seam; a way of joining. It is the power to bring powerful things together, that is a true king. I have never met such a king in my life. Being able to recognize the depths of power in, or of, anything and see where it may go; guiding things together to create that which has never been before, that is a king. It is not the title, the riches, the nobility or the legacy. It is unimpeeding influence. Like a silent awareness, a ghost in the night that is and never needs to be seen."

Gaum breathed deeply as he leaned back. Then with great care he returned the stems to their enclave of soil, pushing on the ground around them ensuring they were deeply settled. He rose carefully and stepped out from the stump. Gaum had a lightness and joy about him now, different from when Taso had first found him in the stump. Gaum stood next to Taso and they looked at the microcosm within the stump.

"Nature has no king," Gaum said, "but it is a kingdom. Every facet, every form of life is a way into, and a part of, that kingdom. The king is in everything, it is everything." Gaum paused again, breathed deeply and whispered, "To be within the flow of that which is of our attention, Hax-Sus."

"Is there a queen?" Taso asked.

Gaum laughed out loud. His voice filled the woods. "I think they are one in the same. I am so glad you are here with me."

Taso noticed that Gaum was not holding the compass, "Where is the spherical compass?" he asked. Gaum reached into a corner of the stump where the grain had formed a sharp contour. Gaum removed the compass. Light reflected off its liquid opening.

The remainder of the day they journeyed on through the woods as the compass guided them. They ate berries and saw trees they had never seen before. When nightfall came the compass compelled them to stop and rest. They found coniferous branches and made themselves each a bed. Taso gazed upon the stars in between the leaves high above.

The trees were silent.

14.

Birdsong in the distance.

    Taso awoke in a warm tight curl within the blanketing of the branches he slept in. His face was cool with moisture. He enjoyed the paired sensation of the damp coolness on his face and the uniform warmth throughout the rest of his body. He saw himself from high above within the folds of branches; the image was a profound sense of well-being. He felt that he was not only close to nature but that he was nature. There was nothing foreign in being in the forest nor in his building a shelter. He did not force nature to comfort him, he found the comfort nature offered him.

    Taso tucked his face into the warmth of his garment and the bristly heat trap of the foliage. He waited for the heat to coat his face, and so fill his entire body. When his face was as warm as his body, he kept his eyes shut then stood and exposed his body to the fullness of the cold morning. He remained there for some time feeling the heat dissipate from his body in a welcoming of the temperature shift. The birdsongs enthralled him.

    Taso opened his eyes to a dense mist that filled the woods. The closest trees appeared as disembodied trunks with their branches and roots consumed by the mist. The texture and depth of their bark muted. They appeared lifeless, more like stone pillars bracing invisible heights and rooted into imperceptible depths. The mist hung as a drapery and moved slowly as transparent curtains of distinct layers passing one another independently. They formed and dissipated at varying speeds. The trees beyond were obscured by the fog.

Taso looked down at his feet. Beneath the branches he stood upon was the forest floor covered in leaves. The outline of his feet radiated into the lines and dimensions of the branches and onto the leaves. Seasons had compacted the leaves with time and shifting temperatures, moisture and light, a continual bonding of decay to release other forms of life. The edge of one leaf was the central stem of another, all within the kaleidoscope of their greens, browns and blacks.

Gaum was not in his own bedding of foliage. Without concern, Taso walked slowly into the fog and among the spectral trees. He listened carefully and retained a peripheral vision to take in as fully as he could the totality of the forest and the fog. He heard more rustlings and flutterings, chirps and the shifting breaths of the mist air. The trees retained their disembodied presence.

In the distance of the mist a flicker of light appeared. It was as a short burst. It did not light the contours of the trees and it appeared as though it were apart from the mist.

Taso walked on in the direction of the light. As he moved towards it, the veils of mist lightened and soon the fog was gone.

Again the single point of light pulsed. Taso became euphoric as he tried to imagine what it could be. Is it alive? A fallen star? A piece of Tor? As his mind filled with questions his footfalls crushed the forest floor's decay and germination. He could not conceive of what could be so distinct and precise an emission of light. As he moved closer to the light it pulsed more irregularly. Then the point of light changed and lengthened. Taso was certain it was magical.

Taso was very close to the light. It was no longer a pulsing point, it was a sustained glimmer. The length of light extended and began to curve. He stopped and looked at. Then a gentle shift in the air came and the curve of light moved.

It was a spider's thread hanging in the air. There was just enough light coming through the fog to highlight it. Taso's heart sank. The mystique of what he believed he was approaching was gone. There was no divine presence, no ethereal epiphany. It was simply a spider's thread. He felt he had guided himself to a false experience.

The visible reaches of the thread curved upwards and into the surrounding mist and distant trees, but from where Taso stood he could not see where either end of the thread was attached. From what he could make of its dimensions, the thread was at least three times as long as the reach of both of his arms. The spider thread gently swayed and then the murk of Taso's disappointment inverted and exploded into a lush realization.

The power of the spider's act flooded his mind, shook his body and churned his emotions. The ability for the spider to refine the thread and connect it between two very distant trees overwhelmed him.

The light reflecting off the thread was not simply an outlining of the thread, it was the reflection of the thread's composition. It was the life of the spider; it was the life of the trees it joined; it was the world in which the thread hung; the distance and composition of Tor. The thread was every event that had brought Taso to this moment and every moment that had formed the event. The spider had created a space in the world that was the synergy of its power and potential with what the world supplied.

The thread swayed a little in the gentle breeze. Taso realized how easily he could break it. With a single finger and gentle pressure, he could bring an end to the scale and magnificence of the architecture of the spider's thread. And yet, he himself could not perform a physical act of the same proportion. There was nothing he could do or create that would match the scale of the spider's creation. He was unable to act; he did not know what to do with the moment. He felt so out of place and at a distance from what was before him. He realized how the choice to interact with the thread was a part of its making, but to break it would not equal the power in its creation.

Taso was filled with the need to enter the thread with his whole body and with all his senses. He needed to go beyond the difference between the thread and the trees. He needed to transcend the seam of their joining and be conducted through all the infinite and magnificent proportions.

How can I experience such a thing? There are great depths to what seems so small. I truly want to see and know how it would feel. But it is impossible.

Taso sat and looked at the spider's thread arcing the air and swaying between the two great trees. He understood what Gaum had meant when he had said, "Roots lead to more roots. Just like questions they go on infintely," and, "I do not understand scale anymore." Taso contemplated these insights observing the spider thread as Tor rose. More of its light came through the tops of the trees and the forest became clearer. But he could still not see where either end of the spider thread was connected. Taso stood.

The forest floor cracked.

15.

Birdsong and footsteps.

Gaum saw no birds as he walked through the fog. He heard their songs and their movements. At times he felt that the melodies and calls were of the fog itself, that the moist thick air was a reverberant body amplifying and transmitting the sounds from far away. He had risen before Taso, and he was so moved by the calm mood and thickness of the fog that he chose to walk in it. The fog was as a new world that had descended and set itself within the forest.

Gaum had walked for some time with the compass but ignored its guidance as he looked for the birds he heard and stayed close to Taso. Until a distant glimmer of light on the forest floor stopped him in his tracks. It was not far from him and it appeared that the ground was glowing. The direction from the compass was not aligned with the strange light. He paused to see if he was sensing the guidance of the compass incorrectly.

He was so fascinated by the unusual light that he ignored the pull of the compass. Moving closer to the light, his excitement grew and his pace quickened. Gaum passed through fog and trees in a direct line with light until he found himself in a community of stones. Each one covered in a lush green moss that was coated with multitudes of water droplets that were capturing and redirecting Tor's light.

Gaum walked among the stones admiring the light that was reflected and refracted by the droplets of water. He came to one stone at the centre of the stones and squatted before it. He held his breath so he would not disturb the balanced positioning of the drops of water. He moved in closer and the features of the moss on the stone opened and deepened into a vast landscape. There was a base of lush green, and like grass it extended over the entire stone with the water droplets nestled in between the blades. Their liquid form was ripe with the green they sat upon.

Amongst the green bedding were stems of varying heights to which one or more drops of water had formed. The droplets were perfectly rounded, their interiors free of any impurities except for the portion of the stem that bisected them. The drops at the tops of the stems dramatically reflected and amplified the light coming down through the trees, beaming as luminous balls of light. Drops further down the stems drew in so much of the surrounding features from the moss, the stems, even the surrounding stones and trees that they had distinct and rich landscapes within them. Gaum wanted to enter each drop of water. He believed that neither one was the same; they were distinct worlds with their own wonders and their own perspectives.

Gaum needed to breathe. He turned his head, exhaled and inhaled, then returned to his meticulous observation of the stone's magnificent moss covering. His eyes went from drop to drop, stem to stem, travelling the surface and finding more unique features. His exploration through the moss landscape required him to move, so again he turned his head and breathed. He walked in a squat to another side of the stone. As he repositioned himself, he felt the movements of the compass shift, directing him away from the community of stones. "Another moment," he thought.

Continuing to scan the minute world of the moss surface, Gaum came upon a particular formation. It was a stem which had been bent by the weight of many droplets of water adhering to it. The curve of the stem was an exact semicircle; the shape so precise that to Gaum it appeared to be half of a complete circle embedded in the moss. All of the droplets on the stem were very close to one another, and by altering his angle slightly, Gaum could look upon the beads of water as a curve of light. He needed to breathe but held it to have more time with the frozen arc of liquid light. The experience remained until the light coming through the trees shifted and the brilliance of the light captured by the droplets of water softened. With the change, Gaum turned his head and breathed.

Gaum sat on the forest floor next to the stone. He was careful not to disrupt the surface of the stone. He looked over the moss landscape as the pushing and pulling from the compass became more noticeable. Its dynamics thickened and drew Gaum's attention from the droplets of water. Gaum held the spherical compass in both hands and stared into its liquid aperture. The light reflected off the opening. He could not see into the dark depths.

What is happening within it? Where will it take us? Why is it taking us? How will this end? The compass continued with its pushes and pulls as Gaum looked over the mossy landscape of the stone. The shimmer of light throughout the water droplets was waning.

Gaum rose. He stabilized himself by placing one hand on the very edge of the stone. Mindful of the moss landscape as he pushed himself up, he moved slowly. But he slipped and the dynamics of the compass moved it out of his hand. To keep hold of it, his hand slid across the top of the stone. It smeared all the droplets as his elbow dug into the moss; pushing through the miniature landscape. He landed against the stone on his side. He was so overcome with the destruction he had caused that he did not think of the shooting pain in his ribs.

He lay there for a moment, awkwardly outstretched over the stone. Looking up at all the other stones he saw their pristine moss landscapes and the multitudes of water droplets that no longer shimmered.

Gaum did not have the heart to look down as he lifted himself off of the remains of the moss landscape. He turned and left the community of stones. The fog had cleared.

The call and response of birdsong filled the forest.

16.

    The thump of the forest floor, cracking twigs and the rustling of debris.

    Tor was high. The fog had completely lifted. When Taso reunited with Gaum he said nothing of the spider thread and Gaum kept his experience in the stone community to himself.

    Gaum held the spherical compass as he lead them through the forest at a leisurely pace. The trees were dense and it required that they continually change direction as the spherical compass was expressing dramatic shifts in its pulling and pushing. There were no straight lines.

    With the trees so close, the forest was dark, and for Taso, it created a mood not unlike the caves in which there was a continual sensation of enclosure and sounds reverberated and moved in unusual ways. Within the density of the trees there was a similar feeling of being surrounded, however, it was a particular kind of sound, not what he would usually listen for. His listening was a growing feeling. He was reaching out more and more with his whole self, his whole presence. Taso found himself straining for sounds he believed were coming from the trees and between them; not the movement of leaves or the creak of branches, it was something else.

Gaum handed the compass to Taso without words. The gesture was natural and happened on its own. Taso felt a strong pull from the compass and less of a pushing sensation.

For some time they moved through the woods with the compass guiding Taso until they came to a very distinct curve in the line of trees. The compass guided them precisely along it. It was the first time Taso had the sensations of the spherical compass aligning so directly with what his eyes saw.

As they rounded the curved path through the trees they came upon a clearing ringed by trees of the same kind. At its center was a large stone embedded in the ground. It was black and had a very even top. The light coming through the tops of the trees fell right upon the stone. It was a powerful place with a simultaneous feeling of lift and depth coming from it. The stone felt and looked as though it was either dropped from the sky or that it was growing out of the ground. A sensation that was intensified by the uniform circumference of the trees.

It was very quiet; no sound, no breeze, no birds or rustlings of life from out of the forest. Taso looked at Gaum. He was transfixed by the place and Taso felt a hidden excitement coming from him. They shared a knowing glance.

Taso walked to the centre of the clearing and placed the spherical compass on the stone at the light's centre. He stepped back slowly, watching it carefully until he reached the perimeter of the light coming through the opening of trees. Gaum walked to the edge of the circle of light until he was opposite Taso. They looked at one another and smiled, knowing something was approaching.

The silence deepened as Taso wondered what was to transpire. A breeze rose; a gentle gesture that grew into a high-pitched whistle. Taso and Gaum covered their ears. The pitch then dropped quickly into a deep, thick roar. It was as an earthquake that shook Taso up through his legs. He looked at the sphere. It did not move. He was thrown to the ground by the force of the sound. There was no place to steady himself. He felt the ground beneath him would open as would his whole body. Everything was on the precipice of coming apart.

The spherical compass did not move. Gaum was on the ground, cringing with the depth of the low thundering sounds overtaking his body and his mind. Taso tried to speak but could not.

Taso could not understand why he and Gaum were so violently assailed by the sounds and yet nothing else was moving. What he saw was not what he felt. The sound penetrated and permeated him. It was invisible and becoming everything. He came onto his hands and knees. He looked up and saw Gaum standing and looking at him. Taso wanted to speak, to ask for help. He attempted to reach an arm out to Gaum but he could not move it. The movement within was too overpowering. He wanted to cry but that too would not come. So he let go of trying and let go of finding a way to stop or change what was happening.

Then all violent sensations of division ceased and there was the clear sound of grinding stone. Taso saw Gaum watching the compass. It was spinning around the edge of the stone. Taso stood up and was dazzled by the glimmers of light coming from the compass' opening. It reminded him of watching the compass rotate along the edge of the crater. The sound of grinding stone continued and it was out of place for such an object's movement. Listening, Taso realized that the sound came from within the stone, not from the compass spinning on its surface. And it was not stone rubbing against stone, it was the stone's own internal friction. The compass was amplifying the depth and resonance of the stone's formation. The forces and time that had molded it were reverberating from deep within it.

The spherical compass made two more revolutions of the stone's perimeter before it stopped. Its exterior opened. The water within churned outwards as a minuscule maelstrom. The currents flowing out of the compass were strong, beading off the animal skin and onto the stone.

Water reverberated into a monstrous torrent.

17.

Currents of dark sounding invisible depths.

Then Taso saw smoke,
it sounded like water,
rose and sank.
Seeping, shuddering and rushing,
smoke filled the air,
cloaked the ground,
consumed the trees
and then darkened the world.

Taso was carried up,
high above the realm of smoke,
beyond buildings and spires,
beyond a terran landscape,
to greater darkness.
It was clean and fresh.

A rich black,

a wholesome air,
nourishing.

Then he was thrown down,
into toxic vapours,
he watched floating embers.

His breath took it all in,
choking ash and smoke.

People running,
shadows morphing.

Taso called out
but his throat was cracked
and dry.
He forced sound, words,
he trembled and shook.

His throat was cracked.
The cracking cracked,
and then came fire.

Uncontrollable fire vomited out
from within him.
It bathed the landscape,
buildings, people.
It pushed back the shadows.
Some shadows moving, they were people,
they waited.

The fire plumed
leaving his mouth like a geyser
and then billowing,
it grew as it consumed.

In desperation,
hands to mouth,
"Let it consume me!" he cried,
he screamed, he ached.

Fire trailed over his hands,
some lingered,
held in a field, a looped current,
in his palms.

Again fire over his hands,
again some remained
and then appeared a new light.

In his hands,
now sculpting fire
all of it into his hands
again within it, new light.

A soft pressure,
the back of his hands touched
by the hands of others.

More and more fire

rushed into his hands
within the folds of crack and roar
there is a laughter
a sweet laughter, child-like,
and then it all became another light.

He held a magnificent brilliance.
An infinite, luminescent ocean in his hands,
all the fire rolled into that other light.
Taso was taken along with it.

The sound was a conduit.

18.

Currents of invisible depths sounding dark.

Then Gaum saw water,
it rushed and cracked,
a knotting and twisting.

Silver lines came from the ground,
straight,
vertical, horizontal.

A frozen measuring, the lines glowed.
Glowed again,
lengthened in all directions,
filled space,
a grid.

All dimension
a luminous grid.

High above,
high in pitch,
a gentle amorphous call.

Gaum looked up
nothing else but the lines, the grid.
He gripped a line,
placed a foot,
ascended.
He climbed to the sound.

Still the high pitch, high above.
Climbing and climbing.
He looked up.
Three pairs of feet,
dangling off the edge of a line.

He climbed further still.

Height dissipated,
direction's purpose waned.
Frustrated,
he could not reach the sound,
he waited on the grid.

He rested his head on the line he held
breathing in and out,
the line began to soften.
It disintegrated, became particles.
As a dust floating

into his mouth,
his nose,
his eyes.

Then the entire lattice work gave way,
its extent, its mass,
absorbed by Gaum.

Until within him,
only a darkness
inhabited by a dissolved luminescence.

He begins to float,
there is a laughter
a sweet laughter, child-like,
and then an unseen dynamic
adds a turning.

Gaum tries to stabilize,
right himself,
but there is nothing
to affix sight
to see up or down.

And then the light inside,
the collapsed lattice,
begins to inhale him.

He is now a dusting,
from within,

he separates,
into minuscule relations.

He does not feel an unhinging
but knows it is happening.

Gaum is becoming no more.

His hands come to his belly
to hold what he can
together.

It is a light within,
then Gaum heard his implosion.

Gaum opened his eyes to the light coming through the branches and leaves high above. The greens so vibrant, the blues so calming. His whole body hummed with a soft tingling sensation. He rolled to one side and sat up. He could see Taso across from him at the edge of the light beaming through the trees, lying as he had before the nameless experience. Gaum stood up slowly, the physical sensation of his body gradually returning. He looked to the stone at the center of the clearing. The spherical compass rested as it had been when Taso first placed it on the stone; it was whole. There was no water on the stone. Gaum stepped beyond the threshold of shadow from where his whole experience had originated. Daylight had not shifted, the experience must have transpired for only a couple of minutes, and yet, it seemed he carried hours.

He walked to the stone. The sunlight grounded his body and its place in the physical world. He reached for the compass and delicately lifted it with his thumb and middle finger. Taso had risen. He too was amazed that the compass was still whole.

Gaum held the compass up so Taso could see it. Taso crossed into the light at the clearing's centre. Gaum handed him the compass. It felt dormant, no pushing or pulling, only the physical texture of its surface and the weight of the water inside.

A breeze moved the leaves of the encircling trees.

19.

A silent departure.

Gaum and Taso continued their journey through the woods. They had moved through, and been moved by, an amorphous clarity. Neither of them felt capable of sharing their experience with the other. They could not relate in words their singular experience and with each step through the lush green of trees and the cushioning earth beneath their feet, the details of their experiences drifted further and further from their recollection. And yet, with the departure of the images, the sensations and the revelations there remained a deeper knowing of something very important and invigorating. However, they could not name it or seize upon it with any sensation. It was as a shadow in the dark.

Taso held the spherical compass in one hand. For the first time since it was fashioned by Gaum, it felt as a simple container of water. None of its initial and cultivated attributes remained; the pushing and pulling, its vaporous and transparent guidance, had all ceased. After his experience at the stone in the clearing, the compass weighed him back into the world. It had guided Taso and Gaum to and through so much, and now, after so profound an experience that was bizarre and fantastic, with the memory of it slipping away, the compass was a simple weight bringing him back into a particular perspective of the world. It was how the world had been to him physically. But that knowing of the world was unlike it had ever been and was no longer the world entire.

As they strolled on, admiring the high reaches of the trees and the deep smell of earth and plant life, they recognised a change in the air. A fragrance and taste that was distinct from the air of the trees and the land. It was pungent, a dense mixture that was at once old and new, but very different from the forest. Taso was overcome with the aromas. He had never smelled or tasted such a mixture. He stopped, closed his eyes and waited for the air currents to send him more. Another waft of air came, and in his mind he saw currents of dark. Taso felt a brief correlation to the remaining elements of his experience in the clearing. He opened his eyes. The colours of the forest flooded in and further ahead he saw Gaum looking up into the trees.

Taso came to Gaum's side and looked up. The branches were different. They were unlike other trees he had seen. Even in their infinite variations, tree branches always depict their central radiation; they open out towards the sky. They lengthen and reach, and even if they form peculiar paths in their growth, the essence of their center is always present.

But these trees depicted a force upon them, one which they had bore consistently. The trees had been molded so that their branches were pointed back into the woods. It looked as though the branches had sought refuge among the other tress. Another centre was imposing itself on them.

They resumed their journey. They were moving closer and closer to what the branches were attempting to avoid. An immense presence was growing. Step after step it felt closer until the presence became a deep and distant lumbering oscillation.

Taso looked at Gaum; he was smiling.

"Is it the sea?" Taso said with a gentle voice.

"Yes!" Gaum responded in an enthusiastic whisper.

Taso's excitement came in the cradle of an equal calm. He had never seen the sea, but after all his experiences, the caves, the crater and the stone clearing, he felt that he knew the sea very well. It was a power in the world that he did not have to succumb to in fear. He could be nourished and guided by its nature.

Taso felt the smooth round surface of the compass and the subtle movements of the water inside. He held it up and looked at the the aperture. It was still a dark liquid surface. Taso touched the water of the opening. Even though the guiding pushes and pulls were no longer present as before; the pressure of his touch left no moisture on his finger.

Walking side by side, Gaum and Taso observed the tree tops and smelled the air. The compass found itself in Gaum's hand; it was a natural and elegant exchange. The trees thinned, and the immense stillness of the sea was before them.

A calm hushed presence.

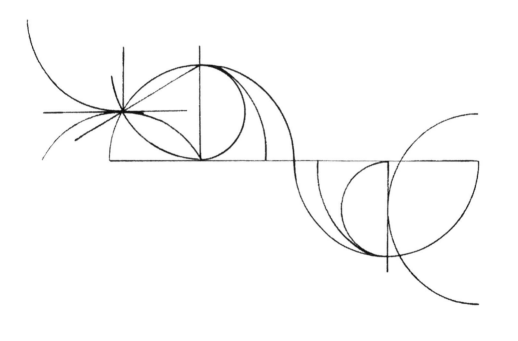

20.

The crunch of the forest floor.

Taso and Gaum stood in between two great trees that marked the end of the forest and the beginning of a rocky beach.

The trees stood as a row of pillars with their roots extending beyond the forest floor and onto the beach. Beyond, the sea looked like an undisturbed mirror reflecting the clouds it met at the horizon. Taso felt the penetrating presence of the water as a silence entering him.

Gaum and Taso smiled at one another. Gaum motioned Taso to lead the way.

Leaving the absorbent base of the forest floor, Taso stepped on to the stoney surface of the beach. He walked measuredly from one stone to another, ensuring he did not make too much noise as he wanted to avoid disturbing the serenity the sea projected. The stones, being of the same relative size, supported his footing equally yet he considered each one a singular encapsulation of compacted time and space.

Taso stopped walking and balanced himself on two stones. "I have never seen the sea," he whispered.

His voice came from out of the sea's calm, formed from each gesture of its currents touching the air and every undulation of its smooth rolling tide. The air smells so strong. I can taste it on my lips.

Taso became euphoric and leapt from stone to stone. It was a suppleness he had never experienced before. He landed assuredly with each step causing the stones to crack and grind. The rhythm carried out towards the sea. As he came close to the water's edge he realized he was not thinking about what he was doing. The need to walk with care filled his mind and whipped through his body. The elegance of his movements slipped and he fell.

Taso landed on his hands and knees. As he fell, he almost cupped his hands towards his belly just as Gaum had taught him to do when they first crossed the plains. The impact of his fall reverberated through his teeth and went clear to the back of his head. All his bones echoed a marrow-deep wince. He looked back to the stones he had overturned and the exposed damp sand. Insects scattered, moving erratically; they were a blur as they concealed themselves within the depths of the beach to overcome the cataclysmic disturbance. Taso's presence had reformatted and impacted everything about him. He imagined a pebble breaking the still surface of water and descending into a sandy bottom, the particles forced up and carried in a gentle current.

Taso rose slowly with the guilt of the image and the ache in his wrists and knees. He resumed his journey across the stones with a heightened sensitivity. I will be more careful.

Gaum stepped from the shade of the trees and into the soft light of the clouded sky, free of the density of earth and the lengthening presence of the root consciousness of the trees. He moved out onto the stones and under the grey tinted clouds. It had been quite some time since he had last been to the sea. He was submerged in its aromas as he walked out on the stone beach. His repeated steps upon the smooth stones reminded him of the spherical compass and he felt a calm call from its watery depths. But there was none of its guiding pushes or pulls.

Gaum knelt and examined the stones. He found a space among them and gently placed the spherical compass with its water aperture facing downwards. It rested snuggly. "As a puzzle piece," Gaum whispered, as he marvelled at the harmony of the compass among the stones with its vellum tint so much like the colouring of the stones around it. "I wish I knew the entire image. I wish I knew my contribution." He laughed to himself. "There is always more. Hax-Sus." Gaum rose leaving the spherical compass where it lay.

Taso made his way to the shoreline. From stone to stone he deepened his step into the totality of each stone's mass and dimension. He continued on in this way of feeling and intention until he reached the shoreline. The tide gently churned over itself. Taso squatted to be close to its momentum. It is like breathing.

The bottom was sandy, a loose and unsettled foundation unlike the solid terrain of the caves, the plains and the forest. Taso looked deeply into the water. It was a cloud of particles, grains of sand that manifested the wearing away and reconstitution of the sea and its shores. In his mind Taso saw the grains sinking deeper into the ocean or floating apart revealing an inconceivable abyss.

Taso wanted to know of those depths and relationships without disturbing them, just as he wanted to enter the spider's thread back in the forest. Yet, he wanted to avoid what he had just done to the stones on the beach. He felt anxiety at the prospect of entering the sea. This surprised him. After his experience with the spherical compass in the clearing, surviving the attack on the kingdom and the journey through the caves, he thought it peculiar that to simply step into the sea would be so frightening. "Hax-Sus," he whispered.

Gaum looked out to the sea, taking in its momentous expanse as he made his way over the stones. With each step, supported by two or three stones at a time, he absorbed more and more of the cloud-contained calm of the sea. The whole world was soft and gentle. Gaum stopped. He recognized that his calm harboured an anxiety. He waited to see if it would fully pronounce itself. He looked back to where he had left the spherical compass and was unable to recognize it from amongst the stones.

Standing at the edge of the sea, Taso looked up to the clouds. They were as they had been that first morning of their journey across the plains. Focusing on the horizon, Taso felt that the sea and the clouds were mutually reflective; they were superimposed on to one another. What is it like to be in the sea or to be in the sky?

Taso's anxiety to enter the sea now encapsulated the clouds and the sky beyond it. He felt in between them and that there is nowhere to go without causing unrest, harm, pain or fear. "How can I move through the world without upsetting it, without being upset?" he whispered, and remembered his euphoria when moving from stone stone, and then the calm calculated way he moved after his fall. Can I be both?

Taso stepped into the sea. It was cold and it electrified his senses, making everything sharper, closer and immediate. He sank a little into the sandy bottom with every step, having to forcibly extract his feet so as not to lose his balance. The water darkened with rising sand that swirled and churned. The reflection of the clouds above deepened the complexity of what Taso saw and he was mesmerized by its beauty.

Gaum watched Taso walk out into the sea. He was anxious. "It is the seam," he whispered, "the boundary between our fragility and vitality."

Gaum walked to the shoreline. He looked down at the gentle movements of the tide and turned his gaze along the smooth curve of the shoreline. He followed it until he reached the horizon. "The next threshold, the next guide," he whispered.

Taso was knee-deep in the water and positioned his hands the way Gaum had shown him at the beginning of their journey across the plains. It felt like an old knowledge, something he had learned long ago for which he had found a new application. He felt heat and tingling sensations. They intensified and he looked down. He saw no light.

Taso looked out to the horizon and felt a lift from between his hands. He allowed his arms to slowly rise, keeping his hands in their relative position. When his hands were in his line of sight, he brought his fingertips together forming a sphere with his hands. The meeting of his fingers formed a seal. The joining of it coursed through his fingers, his hands, his arms and throughout his whole body. He felt a vibrant unity. "Hax-Sus," he whispered.

Looking into his hands, Taso saw the clouded sky and the reflective sea. The horizon marked the vertical point through his hands. The unity Taso felt coursing through his body, he saw within the sphere of his hands. As he exhaled he gently separated his fingers, allowing what they contained to be released. The sky ignited and then the boom of a thunderclap. With the decaying echoes, rain fell. Taso closed his eyes and craned his head back. The cool droplets peppered his face.

The grey stones at Gaum's feet darkened with the falling rain. The seawater in between the stones burst with concentric circles impeded by the surrounding stones. Circles bounded by spheres, he thought.

Taso opened his eyes. Droplets fell in quick arcs around him and upon him; some came very close to his eyes. Taso watched the falling rain until two drops struck both eyes simultaneously. He blinked away the liquid chill and the experience refreshed his sight.

Gaum held out a hand and cupped it. The cold raindrops met the lines in his hands. Gradually, some of the drops followed the lines and coursed into his palm. Soon there was a small pool; raindrops struck its surface animating its calm shallow depths.

Taso watched the concentric circles upon the sea becoming and succumbing to one another as a chorus. Then he looked out to the horizon.

The world droned and pulsed.

Part II

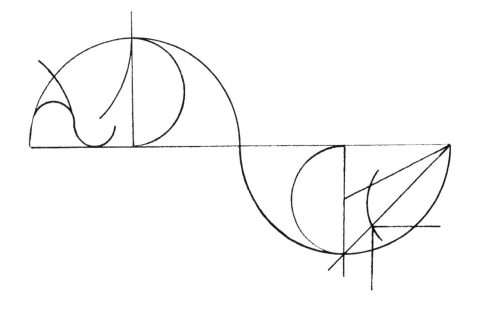

1.

A dark rhythm.

Holna dreamed of currents. Gradually the ripples and swirls in her mind became the sound of a rolling tide and then a cracking. She opened her eyes to the flames of a small fire. Beyond was a rocky shoreline extending to an early morning horizon partitioning the clouded sky and the calm sea. There was no breeze and only two voices: the ocean sounding its shores, the fire sounding its heights.

Holna did not know where she was. Her most recent memory was of the small boat she had taken alone days ago. How did I get here?

She was cold, wet and lying on a foreign rocky shore, yet she felt a smooth surface beneath her. She reached out with her hand and felt a round metallic shape within her grasp. What she saw, felt and heard did not coincide with each other. Holna sat up and looked around: an ocean, a rocky beach, a small fire, and beneath her a light brown door, her hand gripping its brass handle.

Holna tried to recall the event or the choice that had brought her to where she was. She shuddered with memory and her hands went to her heart. It was still there, she felt its edges. It is still tied to my chest. I did not lose it.

Holna reached for her sword, it was not slung to her back. She looked beyond the perimeter of the door and found it resting between the door and the fire. She picked it up and felt the intricate texture of the handle, the sensation brought her comfort. She stood up and strapped it to her waist. The door sounded the unevenness of the stones beneath like a mob knocking to get in or out.

Holna wrapped her arms around herself, enveloping what she carried and drawing in the heat that wanted to leave her. The door pounded and rattled as she stepped off it and onto the stoney beach. She walked to the shore and looked out to the sea. There was no sign of the boat she had used out on the water. Tor, the sun, was behind clouds and it was still midday. She remembered the head monk's words, "Walk with Tor, follow its path without exception until it turns to stone. Please, for me."

She shivered at the memory of his voice. "Me."

Holna wanted to immediately continue on the path of his request. But as her will rose fatigue overtook her. She was too tired and needed rest. The anxiety of not continuing on filled her chest. She beat and rubbed her arms in a self-embrace trying to quell the emotional discomfort. Her breath quickened, she struggled to breathe deeply, when she did the anxiety subsided. She was not accustomed to such feelings. This is not me. "Me" echoed on unbidden.

Holna turned back to the fire and looked beyond the flames to the edge of the rocky beach and the treeline that lead into a forest. She walked towards the fire, intending to rejuvenate the dwindling flames, when she spotted movement within the trees of the forest. She drew her sword and deepened her stance in a single gesture. She breathed deep as she saw a young man. He was ragged, his hair matted, dirt on his face, and he wore a long tattered robe. He was carrying wood. The young man looked at her with soft eyes and a calm expression.

They looked at one another for a moment. The young man's expression did not shift as he turned, dropped the wood and walked back into the dark of the woods. Holna did not move. Her vision went wide, and stretching out with all sensation, she waited for any change in the forest in front of her. The young man was gone and there was no sign of anyone else.

Holna waited a little longer, unmoving and alert. Satisfied that he was gone, she sheathed her sword and turned to the fire. It was only smoke and embers now. She took wood set by the fire and added it to the flames. Did he do this? She noticed her small pack near the fire. She went to it and then sat on the door; again it knocked. She opened up her pack. Nothing had been taken; the dried venison, her face paint and the scarring knife were there as they had been from the beginning of her journey across the sea.

Holna put down her pack and looked again to the woods. Who was that man? The trees are different here. Where am I? She looked into the fire and thought of the head monk. She had left him during the attack on the monastery. He was so still, sitting and waiting for their aggressors to come and storm the prayer room. Holna had never seen anyone meet their death that way.

Thinking of the young man she had seen, she removed her sword and placed it across her lap. A show of strength often avoids its use. Looking out to the sea, she decided to rest for the day and spend the night on the beach. In the morning she would continue her journey following Tor.

As tired as she was, if the young man returned she knew she could handle him. He looked like a hermit, so most likely he was alone and not much of a threat to her. Holna felt the cold again and rubbed her arms. It would be some time before her leather clothing would dry. How did I get here? Where is the boat? Her anxiety resumed with the cold creeping in on her.

Holna shivered and put her hands out to the fire. Holding them in front of the flames, she noticed how old her hands looked. The leather of the sleeves around her thumb was the same texture as her skin, only a little darker in colour. She put more wood on the fire and sat a little closer to the flames.

Holna straightened her posture and closed her eyes. She listened to the fire as it cracked, spit and roared. She went into meditation. It had been sometime since she had followed her breath within.

The sea's liquid pulse rolled in and out.

2.

Flint strikes steel.

A soft light.
Holna stands before the head monk,
seated, his expression bare.
The smell of incense, an aroma of metal,
flickering candle light, an illusion of movement.

The head monk rises,
disrobes.
Holna cannot tell if he is male or female.
"Me," the head monk says,
the word echoes and reechoes.
It grows and grows thickening the air.
It churns and expands,
now a hurricane spinning
it wants to come inside.

The room and then the monastery are broken,

torn up,
taken in the wind.

Holna and the head monk stand facing one another
in a great black void
spinning and churning.

The head monk points at Holna,
his finger bleeds a stream of black ink,
it covers Holna.
The ink pools,
coursing into symbols,
they sink into her skin.

The ink burns,
her body rips, tears,
gnawing flesh
it is deafening.

Holna gasped out of sleep. Her body, inside and out, was rife with violent tingling. Her heart raced and her chest ached.

Holna sat up and touched the ground, her clothes, her sword, anything to deepen the sensations of the physical world into her body. Soon the discomfort subsided and the tingling sensations faded. Clutching her sword, she looked out to the sea. Gradually her breath became tranquil and expansive. The same calm waters had carried her for many days, but rarely had they instilled the calm she now felt.

Holna looked to the fire, it was smoldering embers and charred black remains. She had slept throughout the night and was rested, yet waking as she had so violently, instilled fatigue in her. She was eager to carry on with her journey. She needed to move beyond her rude awakening. She opened her pack and ate a small piece of venison. As she ate, she recalled her dream as though she had bit into memory itself and opened it up, releasing the flavour of images and sounds from the dream. It was upsetting so she returned the venison to her pack and decided to eat later.

Holna strapped her sword to her waist, her pack to her back, then walked to the treeline of the forest. The trees were very different here, she had never seen trees as these before. Their trunks were thick and they towered high above. Their branches had been pushed back in towards the forest. Looking beyond the treeline, Holna could see that even taller trees stood in the woods. The trees also felt different. She could not tell why, but they were somehow inviting and mysterious.

At the treeline, exposed roots from the eroded soil twisted out onto the rocks of the beach. Holna grabbed the roots for support and in two steps was on to the forest floor. She looked back, the last embers of the fire smoked and the door lay close by.

Holna watched Tor's ascent. "Walk with Tor." The head monk's delicate voice came to her and she began to walk in alignment with it.

To move through a dense forest and follow Tor would be challenging and tedious. This bothered Holna as she preferred her quicker natural walking pace. Not only because of her stride, she was one of the tallest people in her tribe, but because it was in her nature to walk quickly. She always had. When she walked she used her whole body: pumping her arms, stepping firmly and standing tall. She most enjoyed climbing mountains, because for every step she needed her whole body and for her this was the most satisfying walk because it meant she was gaining height. When she would look back during a climb she could see what she had crossed. Looking back from a mountain view would either show her path or give a view beyond it. When she had looked back on her path across the ocean, there was no sense of this. It looked the same from either shore and its surface was a continuity of change with no tangible reference points.

As Holna entered the forest, smelling and tasting the shift in sea air to forest air, she listened to the gentle diminishment of the waves of the sea behind her and the growing sonic landscape of the woods. She looked back and saw the ocean framed by two trees. Tor's light glinted off of the ocean's surface. It was so bright that she had to look away. She turned her gaze back into the depths of the woods. Once the shadowed soothing dark of the forest helped her regain her sight, she examined the high reaches of the trees.

Even beyond the treeline, the trees had hard and clear scars of the wind. Holna imagined that during storms the trees were heavily battered. She paused to look carefully at one particular tree. The exposed wood of the trunk and branches had intriguing swirling patterns. Marks from within, the internal scars of growth.

Holna had reached the shore with a fortunate ease. How did I get here? Should I be here? All she remembered was that after days on the sea, one night her sleep was breached. There was a peculiar sound. She did not really know if it had been a sound outside of her, or one she had imagined from within. It was difficult for her to say what it had been. It seemed to be a mixture of water, wood, voices and other indiscernible high and low sounds. None revealed any clarity as to what had happened or why. That sound had woken her and preceded her loss of memory and her unconsciousness. Beyond it there was nothing else until she woke on the beach.

Eventually the trees changed and showed no more signs of the ocean air's weathering effects. The aromas of foliage deepened as the smell of the sea disappeared. Holna slowed her pace. The trees were so thick and high, nothing like those of the forests of her mountain home. She stopped and touched one of the trunks and smelled the bark. It was a sharp smell, pleasant but unusual. The sounds of the forest were also different: the bird song, the wood of the forest floor cracking and cushioning her steps. She moved on, touching one tree after another. Often she would stop and look up at the canopy high above, assessing Tor's position and trajectory.

Holna found these woods soothing, even though they were so different to the forest of her tribal territory. She had not been able to walk in woods of any kind for some time. And this was the second time she was in such a foreign place.

When she was sent to stay with the monks was the first time she was in a truly foreign environment. She found the monastery to be very stifling and she felt trapped behind the high walls. Even though there was a type of peace there - the gentleness of the monks, the care with which they kept the monastery - there were still walls that surrounded the entire compound. Holna continually felt that restriction.

In the first month of her assignment to the monastery, she had had a peculiar experience. Holna observed with great care the lives of the monks; it enabled her to better protect the head monk as it was his life she had been charged with protecting. One afternoon, she watched a monk sweeping an area of the large courtyard. Stroke after measured stroke, he swept dried leaves that had fallen on the grey, flat stones. Holna observed the monk sweep with great care and patience. She found the process very hypnotic at first. Not only because of the monk's serene and focused movements, but also because of the sound of the broom on the stone floor of the courtyard. As Holna continued to watch, she went into a deep calm. But when the monk had reached a corner of the courtyard, he entered the shadow of the outer wall that surrounded the monastery. As he entered the darkly shadowed corner, the monk was barely visible. It was as though he had entered a cave though Holna could still hear his broom sweeping. She was overcome with a rage, like a caged animal and she was suddenly reminded of how she felt trapped in the monastery. Her breath became quick and her chest and throat tightened. The sensation surprised her and she turned away from what she saw.

When she had calmed down, Holna looked back at the monk and he was carrying the leaves he had swept. They rested in his hands like corpses. The monk walked passed her and said nothing as he smiled at her. Holna looked on to the dark corner of the monastery. What is life, what is death? she had wondered.

Holna had learned that for the monks, life and death were an impossible relationship to understand, it is simply the way of things that one must accept. But in her tribe, life and death were the tools of the gods. It was up to each person to prove themselves; this was known as the scars of life. The marking of skin is painful, and depending on the kind of cut, it is an injury that stays with you and becomes a part of you. Through your scars you tell the story of your life, and because it is cut into you, you cannot lie about it. Through the scars the gods can see into you, and so know your truth; what is within you and what you did needed to harmonize. The scars of life are a blessing so that the gods will honour you with eternal life, power and riches of the afterlife. All of these may be given if you carried powerful scars. It is your actions and choices with life and death that formed these scars. One must strive to gain the greatest scars. Watching the monk sweep was the first time Holna questioned life and death in this way.

Holna moved on through the woods and realized her reverie was slowing her down. She stopped touching the trees and picked up her pace. She continued to stop often so she could orient herself to Tor. The meandering path she was taking through the woods was disorienting.

On the sea it was easier to focus upon Tor. Apart from the odd cloud cover, it was a clear and evident compass. It was only at night that she was concerned with her direction. She would lie in the bottom of the boat, look up at the stars and feel anxious that they could not guide her as

Tor did. Certainly they moved across the sky in the same direction, but they all held different positions and the head monk had said to follow Tor "without exception." Eventually, as Holna watched the stars, the waves lapping at the side of the boat and the rocking movement would lull her to sleep. Then she would awaken in daylight with Tor just above the horizon.

Walking on through the woods, try as Holna did to focus on her path, the need to recall her journey in the boat kept coming into her mind. What happened? All memories ceased with that indescribable sound and then awakening on the beach in front of the fire on a door. There was no arrival, only a new place. Why a door? Where did it come from?

Unable to remember her journey left Holna feeling uneasy. In her tribe it was important to be able to recount where you had been and what you had done. The scars were a part of this. Just as you needed to show them to the gods, you needed to show others your value. This was why walking with her whole self was so important to Holna, it was how she knew where she was.

The monks spoke very little. They believed that one must choose words carefully. But for Holna it was not simply that they did not speak very much, but they seemed to be holding back. If she asked a monk a question, especially if it was about their opinion, they seldom, if ever, answered. She found this to be unnatural.

Holna looked up at the forest canopy to see Tor's position. The branches were very close. The spaces between the branches reminded her of the scars of life, her dream and the sharp tingling sensations in her body when she awoke. She had never experienced peculiar, subtle sensations in her body until she had begun meditating. The head monk had taught her meditation after a few months at the monastery. It had been his suggestion. Holna was surprised at the offering. At first she had refused because she assumed that it would distract her from her purpose of protecting the head monk. But he had said, "To be still, to move, these are the same." The idea intrigued her and so she acquiesced.

Holna meditated everyday, but only at times when she was confident of the head monk's safety. Her first three attempts were very frustrating, on the fourth, her mind went from thought to thought, image to image and then she suddenly was aware of an odd movement and heat over her back. And with it were dark currents, within and around her. It felt like a wind or breeze. It was such a strong sensation that she opened her eyes and checked for airflow behind her. She found nothing and then within moments of returning to her meditation, the sensation returned, and with it, the dark currents. She was able to focus on the strange movement, and when she finished meditating she felt a calmness and wellness she had never felt before. As she continued to meditate other subtle sensations would arise. It was never the same, sometimes, very little would seem to occur. In fact, there were times when meditating was so still that she would fall asleep. She had asked the head monk about this. "That is very interesting, you must be tired." he had said.

Holna took offence at his words, fatigue did not dictate her life. A few days before the attack on the monastery she had stopped meditating altogether. It was not until her arrival at the mysterious beach that she had meditated again. It seemed appropriate.

But her dream of the head monk and waking to the sharp tingling sensations was new - she did not like it. And it happened in sleep, not in meditation. Holna felt an anxiety towards sleep she had never had before. What happens when we sleep? Why do we need to sleep?

One of the young monks had said that meditation has some dangers and that she should be careful with it. At the time, she believed he was playing with her, trying to deepen a mystery that was not real. Now she did not know what sleep or dreaming was. If she could have such experiences coming out of sleep, perhaps there were some dangers in meditation, and for that matter, sleep itself.

Holna stopped walking and looked up to the canopy. Tor was obscured by a dense array of branches. She removed her pack and ate venison as she waited for Tor's guidance.

The chewing of flesh permeated the forest.

3.

The forest floor cracked.

Holna stooped down as she gripped the handle of her sword; there was movement far ahead. She hid behind a tree and watched a shadow among the trees. Eventually she could make out an arm, fingers, and then the shape of a person. The figure dropped down. There was the sound of moving leaves which were then thrown up into the air. The figure jumped up, ran for a few steps and then ducked down again. Holna quietly approached as she monitored the figure's erratic movements and maintained her alignment with Tor.

At first it was awkward to match her positioning within those two references: one terran, the other celestial. But as she continued on, she recognized how the figure was moving away from her while keeping the same alignment with Tor. She found the pace tedious and frustrating. She clenched her jaw. Why not kill him and be done with it?

She stopped in her tracks. The thought confused her as her heart seethed. There were more voices in the thought. She brought her hand to her heart feeling what she carried. The head monk's voice came clearly,

"Please, for me." It echoed. As with the killing thought, there were more voices appearing within "me."

Holna was not quick to kill. But what she felt in her heart, "me," urged her on as a chorus reaching out to her and calling her to action.

Again the figure she was following stayed in one place, now jumping up and down, disturbing the ground and leaves. She could not make out what was taking place. By now she was very certain it was the young man she had seen when she was on the beach. Maybe she would only need to scare him off. He was in direct alignment with Tor; she needed a clear path to follow it.

Holna was closer to the unknown man now. He seemed to be highly focused on something in the ground. He is distracted, now is the time. With great speed and light movements, she moved towards him. Drawing her sword, she paused at a tree that was some ten paces away from him. Now Holna was certain, it was the young man she had seen in the forest at the beach. She was certain he had not heard her. She watched him. He was moving the earth and debris of the forest, arranging leaves and branches in patterns she could not quite make out. He said nothing, but his breathing was heavy.

Holna took in a deep breath and watched the young man as he continued to focus on the ground. She brought back her sword and stood upright. She was at least a full head taller than the young man. She let out her battle scream.

The young man turned to her, standing very tall, and raised his tunic showing his genitals. He shook his body like a dying fish. Holna froze at the sight of his display, her battle scream cut dry. She stood there holding her sword drawn back. She was overcome with anger and offence at his actions. The chorus of voices from her heart spoke and then she stepped forward to cut down on him. The young man turned on one foot with ease as he still held up his tunic. He smiled at Holna. She turned around to cut him through the stomach but he stepped back as he dropped his tunic which glanced off her sword and let out a quick *tang*. Then the young man ran off at an incredible speed through the trees. Holna watched him go until she could no longer hear his footfalls and the breaking undergrowth. She lowered her sword wondering who really surprised who.

Holna sheathed her sword. Having seen him more closely, Holna was now certain he was a hermit; young, a tattered tunic, unshaven, with wild unkept hair. She examined the ground he had been focused on. There were a number of shallow holes in the ground with raised edges of earth. There were three and he had been creating a fourth. He had also broken up dried leaves and branches into very fine little paths around the shallow holes.

Unable to discern the young hermit's intentions, Holna realigned herself with Tor and made her way through the forest. She stopped several times and would wait to gauge Tor's direction through the fine network of branches. At times the canopy was so thick that she had to wait and measure the light that fell on the tree trunks or the ground. She would wait long enough to get an approximate angle and then she would move some distance before having to renew the measurement.

When Tor was directly above her, she rested and ate some venison. This was how she moved through the woods throughout the day. Not once after her encounter with the young hermit did she see or hear him.

When evening came, Tor's light barely reached within the forest and the woods grew dark very quickly. It was at this time that Holna came upon a clearing. At its centre was a large stone.

She walked up to the stone in the halo of the last moments of daylight. The stone was as high as her waist and had a flat, even top. She placed her hand on it as daylight vanished. The stone was cool. Is this what the head monk meant? Is this Tor turning to stone?

From the moment the head monk had made his request, Holna was of two minds: stopping and going on. This is what churned and burned in her heart. She did not believe in the lifestyle of the monks, nor their beliefs. Yet at every moment throughout her journey she was conflicted.

Two days before the attack on the monastery, Holna and the head monk were in the prayer room. The other monks had left, completing their afternoon meditation. When they had all departed the head monk motioned Holna to come to him. She stood one step away from him and waited for him to speak. But he said nothing.

Then he looked deeply into her eyes. Holna was about to ask what it was that he wanted, when something appeared in the head monk's eyes. It was a glimmer she felt. Then his hand reached out and touched her heart, "Remember?" he whispered.

Her mind was suddenly filled with images, sounds and voices. Her whole body lush with a potent vibrancy. When it had ended she was left with an experience of love she had never known. Now in the clearing of the unknown woods she was travelling through, the potency of that memory filled Holna's mind, her heart and her body as it had on that day. She pounded her fist into the stone. The memories recoiled with the harsh pain that sharply drove through the bones of her fist and she was fully brought back to the dark of the woods. No, this is not Tor turning to stone.

Holna considered where to sleep; on the stone would be too vulnerable so she crouched down to one side of the stone and decided to sleep there for the night. She removed her pack and drew her sword from her belt. She curled her arms around her sword as she rested her head on her pack.

The head monk's voice came to her, "Please, for me," and it echoed on in her mind. Holna recalled the voices telling her to kill the young hermit. Hearing the voices within "me," she tried to clearly identify each voice. It felt like a hunt within her own mind.

The more she sought the clarity of each voice, the more quickly they would retreat back into the whole of the resounding "me." As animals will retreat and elude the hunter, Holna felt that the voices themselves were willfully avoiding her. The experience brought on a chill with memories of winter hunts.

Her tribe would bring down what they could in winter. Hunting was the profound relationship of finding life in life. In most of the seasons, the woods are so active everything is growing and changing, living and dying. Winter is different from every other season because you are hunting a very particular life in the midst of the life dormancy of the forest.

On Holna's first hunt she had brought down a large deer. She remembered the pause before she used her bow and the great space in between the release of the arrow and it striking the deer. The feeling of the balance of accuracy and uncertainty forever stayed with her. The shot was clean and the animal dropped to the ground. As she had stood over its body, Holna had contemplated how she would not see that deer walk through the forest again. But even if it did, it would do everything it could to avoid her. To kill it was to be as close to it as she could.

The voices within "me" was as hunting an animal in winter but it was an unknown animal. What Holna felt was new and foreign. She did not know how to approach it and to capture it, so it would cease to plague her as it did.

Holna recalled the head monk's hand staying at her heart for two breaths. She did not count them, the breaths counted her and then he pulled his hand away quickly. Why did that happen? She was overcome with dimensions and sensations in her heart she had never known. And then two days later, at night, the attack came. It was then that the head monk had made his request. There was a depth and even a radiance that she did not understand in his request. Holna cradled her sword closer as she laid at the base of the stone. The memories gradually softened to currents of dark that moved her towards sleep.

The air was silent and still.

4.

The gong rang.

It was deep and full,
limitless.

The gong rang again.
It sounds beyond the monastery,
finds,
fills,
the edges of the world,
beyond.

Holna stands in the courtyard of the monastery.
In her right hand the handle of her sword,
in the left, the blade.

She looks down,
both hands are empty.

The gong is grey-brown,
rough,
like earth of a heavily treaded path,
the hands that pounded the metal, bloodied.

The gong rings.
The edges of the world resound.

In one hand, the blade of her sword, in the other, the handle.
"To hold is to be cut,
to cut is to be held," a voice Holna has never heard.

Separation and union,
what is undone,
is new,
is whole.

The gong sounds.
It fills all,
shaking all,
apart.

Holna heard birdsong. She kept her eyes shut tightly as she lingered in the warm curl of sleep. She did not want to get up. Every morning she had risen immediately, often without fully waking up. But for the first time in many years, she felt the need to linger at the edge of sleep.

Her heart became hot and something did not feel right.

With her eyes still shut, Holna rolled away from the stone and onto one knee. She turned as she opened her eyes and drew her sword. The tip pointing steadfast at the young hermit as he sat on the stone.

He did not move as he smiled at Holna. She stood up and rushed at him bringing her sword down upon him. But the young hermit was already off the stone and running into the trees beyond the clearing. Holna watched him go and waited until she could no longer here the crack of the undergrowth. I held back. Ulh that he is. Birdsong came back to her awareness and she sheathed her sword. Only an ulh, a fool, would act this way. I should not have let my guard down. Comfort is not an option now. Not until I finish. She heard the head monk's voice, "Please, for me."

She looked at the stone, then examined the clear line of trees that formed the clearing. In daylight she could see how soothing a place it was. She felt it. That was why I did not want to immediately get up. Her panting subsided and her sense of ease returned. She climbed up on the stone and sat just as the hermit had. She listened to the birds and looked up at the opening of the trees above.

Sitting on the stone she began to feel less and less compelled to go on. She brought her hand to her chest. She felt the shape of what she carried under her clothing. As her finger rubbed a portion of its outline she recalled the attack on the monastery.

She had made her promise to the head monk as their attackers were coming up the stairs to the prayer room. She had leaped from the window, climbed down the three stories, finally jumping into a throng of their attackers. They recoiled at her size and her battle cry. She had killed half a dozen of them before they were able to come at her. But then she was already on her way through a side gate and losing herself in the woods. As she ran, the head monk's words reverberated in her mind, "Follow Tor, for me."

The memory of his words brought a warmth and an ache to her heart. She could still feel his touch at her heart centre; the sensation was an indescribable movement within her that went deep.

Memories of that night were painful and uncomfortable and Holna's sense of ease in the clearing fell away. She leaped from the stone. This place is special. I don't want to leave. But I must continue on.

Then she remembered the calm she felt when hearing the gong in the courtyard of the monastery. She stood there for a moment recalling its deep, soothing tone. All other thoughts and feelings gradually subsided as the profound sonorities filled her more and more.

Holna looked skyward and found Tor's position. Once she gained a sense of its direction, she started off in line with its ascent. It was the same direction that the young hermit had taken in his flight.

As she walked among the trees, Holna continued to hear the gong in her mind. It sounded in its own time, apart from the rhythm of her footfalls. It filled her and encouraged her. She would have flourishes of euphoria from its resonance and so she would dash ahead, slow down and then dash on again. This pattern of movement with Tor continued until there was a crack of branches far ahead of her.

Holna stopped and crouched behind a tree. She drew her sword and waited. She peered around the tree but saw no movement. The cracking sound had a heavy weight to it. Holna kept her sword drawn as she walked on. The handle of her sword always felt good to her, even when she held it in its scabbard. Its wrapped cord was calming and assuring.

Holna moved on from tree to tree, listening for the next sign of her follower's position. She shifted her grip of the handle intensifying the comfort it provided her.

She remembered the first time she had held a sword. She was very young and her mother had placed it in her hands. Then she had stood behind Holna helping her hold the sword with its tip pointed forward. Even with that support, Holna could feel the weight of the sword and the density of the steel. There is nothing else like that feeling. She learned how swords were made and she enjoyed watching the smith pound the blade. Her tribe believed that every strike, its power and its force, put into the steel, stayed within the sword. When you held a sword you held the power of its forging.

Holna paused behind a tree and waited. Still no other sound, not a crack or shifting of the forest around her. She sheathed her sword and walked on at a quick pace. The sound of the gong in her mind returned. She realized that it had been with her all along.

The gong continued within as the forest sounded its own movements.

5.

A breeze rose and moved leaves.

The sound reminded Holna of the tide. She looked up and watched the unmoving branches as the soft breeze made the leaves tremble. The contrast was significant to her in a way she had never realized. She had always loved the forest but seeing trees and woods foreign to her set her mind into a questioning she could not recall ever having. She paused in her journey. How can there be such great stillness supporting so much movement?

Holna recalled a similar thought when she was on the sea in the small boat. Often she would look over the side of the boat and imagine what was within the depths. So often the reflection and movement of the surface of the water would have her imagining all kinds of creatures that she would not have conceived of otherwise. And she would wonder what it was like to be in those depths beneath the surface and what was down there.

On one occasion she saw movement beneath the surface and it appeared to be a large fish. A breeze came, shuddered the surface of the water, obscuring the clarity of what she could see. In that moment it struck

Holna that the surface of the water was distinctly separate from the air above and the water below. The surface was a thin divider and they had no connection or relationship; the air and the water were two different worlds. The surface was of both of them and was neither of them.

A number of times she was tempted to go into the water, even though she could not swim. There had never been a need for it in her life. She had gone into lakes and moved about, washed and played as a child, but she never really knew how to swim.

It was a strange impulse to desire entering the sea. It thrilled her in ways she had not know since she was a child; it was a visceral rush of the mortal risk and the excitement of a new experience. Eventually, she decided against going into the sea, the risks seemed too great.

Again the breeze in the woods came and moved the leaves high above. The branches remained fixed. Looking up at the trees, Holna imagined that the leaves separated the world beneath the branches from the sky above. So now, she was submerged in the forest.

The breeze grew and gently swayed some of the branches as their trunks remained still Do the deep waters of the sea move? What if there is unmoving water, like the branches supporting the leaves? Maybe there is frozen water that holds all the other waters' movements.

Contemplating stillness and movement reminded Holna of the monastery. The monks maintained a stillness and a peace in how they moved and how they lived.

Holna brought her hand to the centre of her chest. She felt the hard edge of what she carried and the memory of the head monk's gentle but penetrating touch. The two were at once unified and very separate. Each had a singular stillness and movement. Where am I going?

A year ago she had never been inside the walls of a monastery, nor had she ever taken a boat, let alone leave shore and cross a sea. So much had changed. It seemed so long ago since she had been hunting with her people or sat with her leader and listened to her wise counsel. Only at her leader's request would Holna have gone without hesitation to stay with the monks as she had.

Holna felt she was being lead by something she could not see or understand, only follow. This was frustrating and uncomfortable. She was aware of a centre within herself that she could not measure. *Will I ever be free of this feeling?*

Another soft breeze came and Holna looked up at the forest canopy. She walked on.

Silent branches held quivering leaves.

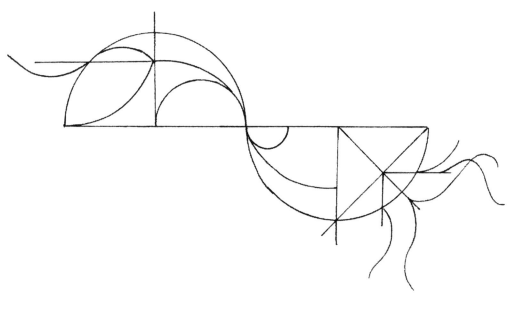

6.

A foreign impact in the woods.

Holna's sword banged against a tree as she leaned into its trunk. She looked up the length of the tree's trunk and how its branches added to the forest canopy. It was midday and Tor was heavily concealed by the branches.

Holna removed her pack. She took out a strip of venison, bit a small portion, and then removed her scarring knife and face paint. She placed them both on top of her pack and looked at them as she ate the remainder of the venison.

It had been more than a year since she had worn any paint. It was for the last tribe battle. Her tribe had been victorious and she had killed twelve men. None of the women from the opposing tribe fought.

The last man she killed held the blade of her sword when she had forced it into his stomach. The blood had gushed from his hands as he tried to keep it from going in deeper or as he tried to pull it out. The look on his face from the pain was not unusual to Holna but she remembered far more vividly the look of freedom in his eyes when he died. She had never seen that before. It had made so strong an impression upon her that she wondered if all those whose last moments she had witnessed had had the same expression. It was not the life leaving the body, it was what he was seeing. He looked through me. I do not know what it was, but his eyes were wide and seemed unlimited. It was as though his eyes were free to see; there was no limit.

Holna picked up the intricately carved paint container. It was made from a tree she had not seen in this forest. Then she placed it back on her pack. She grabbed the scarring knife and felt its weight in her hand. The blade was made of a black stone, that when broken correctly, formed very sharp edges. It could be used as a weapon but in her tribe it had a different significance. It was the tool of the scars, the evidence of ones life and actions.

Holna rolled back the leather wrist sleeve of her left arm and exposed the skin. In the shade of the tree, she examined the inflammation from her recent scarring. The last time she had cut into her arm was on the sea. It was a single smooth line that she had made, but one she had chosen and done for herself. This was not in keeping with the ways of her tribe. Through life there were familiar scars: first hunt, first battle. But when a scar was for a special or unique event, it needed to be made by the Seer. They were needed to call the gods for the appropriate scar. Holna had no knowledge of anyone having to scar themselves with such events. But she needed a scar.

When the Seer would call for the name of a scar they would go into a trance. They would make odd sounds, their eyes would roll back, they would convulse and sweat. In the trance they became something else; they were neither man nor woman, they were an unknown animal. Then the name of the scar would come to them. They cut the design into the skin and then chanted as they rubbed the ink into the wound.

Holna knew of no mark for where she was now or when she had been on the ocean. But she needed to record the task. *Before I die.*

Holna looked around the foreign woods and nothing gave her an indication of the name of the scar she needed on her skin. She rolled back her sleeve further to reveal the scarring that recorded her last battle. Holna's mother had told her that the reflective black surface of the knife and the black ink were the requirements of the gods so that one may prove oneself to them. "The ink is from the black embers of our fires," her mother had said, "it is where light was made. The stone comes from deep within caves in the ground. It is hard and never burns, yet when broken it reflects light. When you go to the gods your scars are dark but they will be of light."

The new scarring had no ink. It was a single line she had made while in the small boat on the sea. She hesitated to add the ink. What if it is wrong? I cannot sing like the Seer.

Now, as she looked at the inkless scars, her heart began to warm; an ache presented itself deep in her chest very much like the sensation she had when she felt the desire to kill the young hermit. She saw herself shaving off an entire length of her skin. The thought sickened her. She closed her eyes and took a moment to calm herself.

"It must be done now, before my death," she whispered. "I may never have the chance to request the name of the scars from the Seer. I may never go home." She took a couple breaths and made two cuts into her skin that bisected the inkless scar line she had made upon the sea. She stifled the sounds of pain in her throat and breathed deeply.

The trees muffled stone cutting skin.

7.

Birdsong diminished in the quickening dark.

Dusk came as the ground beneath Holna's feet softened. In the dim light she approached the freshly cut stump of a tree. She stopped in her tracks. There were more stumps scattered about other trees in the area and further along she could see the corner of a house. She smelled smoke.

Holna hid behind a tree and waited. There was no visible or audible activity. She drew her sword and quietly moved to another tree, then another. Approaching the house, she could see firelight coming from between the wood boards of a window. She reached the back of the house. In front of it was a fire pit, and beyond, an embankment from where she heard a stream. From inside the house she heard a fire as she listened for any other activity.

The forest darkened as Holna approached the doorway. There was a long piece of fabric over the entrance. She waited and listened. Still, the only sound from within was of a fire. Holna deepened her grip on her sword and pointed its tip at the entrance. She threw back the fabric and rushed in.

No one was inside but the house was lived in and very clean. The house's construction was very different from the huts in her tribe and that of the monastery. There was a clay fireplace with a large fire; the air in the house was so warm and inviting that it compelled her to stay. It was unlike the soothing feelings of the woods, this was very different and she understood it immediately. She was lonely.

Holna had been sent on a journey from a single person's words and she had heard none others since. She had had nothing beyond the company of her own thoughts. Certainly in the past she had spent time alone, but never like this. She had been sent out into the world without knowing who she would encounter. Her sudden departure from the monastery meant there had been no warm tidings and no invitations to return. She took a deep breath of the warm air and the wooden floor creaked as she continued to examine the small house.

In one corner was an assortment of tools. There was a bed, a table and a chair. Over the chair was a beautiful blanket. Holna touched it with great care. She had never felt material like that. It was deep and heavy. She picked it up and examined it more closely in the firelight. It was a lush blue with grey speckling throughout. It seemed so out of place. It was nothing like the material that hung in the doorway and unlike the quality of anything else in the house.

Feeling the texture of the blanket intensified Holna's compulsion to stay. Her heart began to ache and her thoughts wrestled one another. Kill whomever comes. Take the blanket for yourself. Wait for whomever lives here, convince them to let you stay. You would have someone to spend time with. Maybe you could speak with them. You cannot stay, you must continue on. Burn it down, if you cannot have it no one can. The thoughts rolled on.

Holna was not looking forward to spending another night in the woods when she could have shelter and a warm fire. She decided to leave but to take the blanket with her. Surely it would not be a heavy loss to the house's owner.

She went through the clothed doorway as she had entered, sword tip first, running on through the trees in the direction that Tor had set earlier. The very faintest glimmers of daylight remained in the woods. Holna ran hard.

Soon the woods were dark. She came to the base of a tree and decided to spend the night there. She sat cross-legged and wrapped herself in the new-found blanket, her sword unsheathed across her lap. The fabric's immediate warmth contributed to the giddiness she felt from having taken it. She felt she had been gifted by the discovery.

Holna closed her eyes and fell asleep with the handle of her sword in hand.

The click of Holna's sword leaving its scabbard.

The sword draws slowly,
it sounds as an earthquake,
as a wind.

Her tribe,
faces painted,
soft eyes, hard eyes.
The paint comes away,
from soft eyes, hard eyes,
it floats as black currents,
as water,
as smoke.

The black currents fill the air.
The tribe drowns,
standing;
they look as statues in aimless poses,
with indifferent expressions.

There was a fire,
the novices,
the child monks,
their robes began to grow,
as one within the fabric,
they drowned,
standing.

Holna stands in the courtyard of the monastery,
soldiers surround her.
She cuts with her sword,
it touches none of them,
the sound,
the cut,
shakes the air,
shakes the soldiers,
they burst and break, they resound.

Then she is warm.
She is looking up at a beautiful woman.
Holna feels the fabric of the blanket around her.
Its colours start to appear in the lines of the woman's face.

Colours,

shifting patterns,

trace,

obscure,

the woman's face.

They are simple, with meaning,

Holna knows.

Holna needs to cry, she cannot; the woman cries for her.

And then everything cried out.

8.

A crack from out of the woods.

It jolted Holna from her slumber; dark images ushered her into the light of day and the anxiety in her heart.

Setting off in the early light of the morning, she aligned herself with Tor's direction and made her way among the trees as she ate a little venison. She kept the blanket over her shoulders. She felt regal to have such a luxurious drape of fabric over her; the heat it held invigorated her.

Finishing the venison, she wrapped her arms within the cloth and drew the blanket in close to her. As her feet sank into the soft earth of the forest floor, she rubbed the blanket with her fingers. The texture was very soothing. She had never felt anything quite like it.

Recalling the small house she had taken the blanket from, Holna was sure that the blanket not been made there. It did not seem possible to her that anyone living in such a place would be able to make a blanket of this quality. She felt that the blanket had come from some distant place and was perhaps, for the house's occupant, an acquisition by chance as it had been for her. Maybe as a passing stranger in some far-off kingdom they came upon it draped in an open window as its owner had let it air in midday, or a late night encounter between two lovers that were interrupted, one of them running off with the blanket for shelter or to hide their identity. Holna imagined a host of scenarios, a chain of foreign hands and means.

For a moment she felt a sinking feeling for that person's loss of the blanket, but rubbing the fabric in between her fingers quelled her negative feelings. Her attention went to the weight of the fabric and the richness of the heat she felt beneath it. Walking on, her stride widened and she felt as though the blanket was helping her move through the woods.

Holna continued her reverie of the blanket. She imagined its manufacture in a wealthy kingdom. Gold and silver polished and shimmering in the sunlight. Large communities, people of different standings, wealthy and poor. And within all the activity of those people came this blanket. Made by a single person, perhaps at a loom of complex engineering. This blanket came from a place like none other she had seen in any of the cities, communities or tribes she had known, not even in the monastery would a fabric like this be found.

With these images came a confusing feeling of hope and despair. Holna could not place the feeling. Hope and despair for what or why?

Then she realized they were for all people. It was a strange feeling because it was for people of whom she had no knowledge. In the monastery, the monks spoke of the similarity and even the equality of people. But this seemed so odd to her. Men and women are different, peasants cannot be kings, so people do not have the same value. They cannot be equal. Her hand went to her heart, she felt what she carried and the presence of the head monk's touch blossomed in her heart.

There was a cracking of branches behind her. She stopped and crouched. She remained motionless as her emotions and thoughts shifted to the pointed awareness of her surroundings.

The forest was still but Holna knew the young hermit was nearby. She let go of her hold on the blanket. It draped down from her body brushing the forest floor as she slowly unsheathed her sword. She knew he was quick but she felt no real threat from him. Why is he following me?

She listened for his movements. Another crack. He was moving around her. He kept the same relative distance as he circled her. Now and then, within the cracks she heard the ruffling of foliage.

Holna aligned herself with Tor's ascent and with her sword resting on the blanket over her shoulder, she walked on slowly in a crouched position. She listened to the young hermit's movements accompanied by the light brushing of the blanket on the forest floor. The cracks continued maintaining a circular distance around her. This went on for some time. Holna began to feel frustrated by how she was being stalked and contained. She moved more quickly attempting to close the distance between them. But he matched her movements and kept the same distance.

Holna knew that hunting is engaging with an animal that has special qualities. Its limbs, its senses and its meat are all special to that animal as much as its way of life. How an animal lives is not only about what it is but also how you hunt it. In her tribe, certain people were better at hunting certain animals. It was believed that if you could hunt an animal you shared something with it.

But any knowledge or skill in hunting animals was not enough for hunting a person. Because a person thinks and they can make choices you might not expect. Most importantly they can transform. A person can become many things and in the case of her tribe's seer, may become something with no identity, they may become inhuman, an unknown animal. This young hermit did not seem to her to be a seer. He was more likely to be an ulh, this is not like a seer. There are certain rituals and experiences seers must fulfill and overcome. An ulh comes into life hearing different things which have never been heard by others. These sounds come from places unknown and not of this world. She had never met an ulh but this young hermit seemed to be like one as they had been described to her.

Again Holna tried to get closer to the the young hermit. But still he maintained his distance. Perhaps he is hunting me? But she could not imagine why that would be. If a normal person is difficult to understand at times, then how could she understand this ulh's motivations? He appeared to have no weapon and seemed unwilling to fight.

Holna stood up. I will no longer do this, she thought as she sheathed her sword. Let him follow me, there is nothing to come of it. He is harmless.

She wrapped the blanket around her and walked tall. Her gait was moderate through the woods as she followed Tor. She rubbed the fabric of the blanket between her fingers. The cracks and shifting of the forest floor beneath her feet were echoed now and then by her invisible follower circling her.

The sounds of a centre and a perimeter.

9.

The trees thinned and the wind faintly whistled.

The forest floor rose and Holna came to the edge of a path. It was formed of small crushed stones and she stood at the midpoint of where the path curved. It lead out of the woods on a direct line with Tor's direction through the sky.

Holna stepped onto the path. The sound of shifting stones and the hard resistance under her feet was so different than the forest floor. Until this step, the forest had been a yielding base, now with this rocky path the support beneath her was much more rigid. As she walked along the path she looked at the trees that framed the threshold to a great expanse of grass. Her footfalls echoed amongst the trees and into the surrounding woods.

Walking the stone path reminded her of the first time she approached the monastery. There was a similar path that lead through the forest to its front gate. When she had reached the gate and saw the extent of the outer wall she felt enclosed. Now in these foreign woods, she walked a similar path to an opening.

Holna's pace quickened as she neared the edge of the forest. She stepped beyond the line of trees that demarked the end of the woods and the beginning of a vast plain. She took a deep breath as she stood in the shade of the trees. The air was so fresh and the world looked like it was only grass.

Holna scanned the horizon; from left to right she looked for features. When her eyes came back to the woods and settled on the treeline, she noticed a small structure. It appeared to be a tiny house elevated off the ground.

Holna stepped off the stone path and went to the tiny house. As she walked her hand went to her chest. The house was a shrine of wood mounted on a stone base. There were decayed flowers and food at the feet of a statue with many limbs inside the shrine. It had a split face: one side grotesque and angry, the other calm and content. The two faces met and morphed together so they were one. The figure was carved out of a light grey stone.

She had never seen a face such as this one, but it reminded her of the monks. The night of the attack, when she had just entered the surrounding forest of the monastery, she stopped running and looked back. In the courtyard the child monks were gathered. Their faces were as stone, looking up at their captors. Then without a shift in their poise or faces, they were cut down, beheaded and sliced open. She imagined the same fate had befallen all the monks.

Her heart ached and she became so frustrated she paced back and forth in front of the shrine. She clutched what she carried on her chest, pushing it into her heart. Her breath became heavy and forced. Her other hand squeezed the handle of her sword. She looked at the face of the statue. The line of its mouth seamlessly containing tranquility and anger, intensified her state and she was enraged.

Holna turned and screamed at the shrine. Her voice was at once deep and shrill. She kicked over the shrine sending it off the stone base and into the woods. She followed it in its fall, drew her sword and wildly cut into it as it lay on the ground. Her eyes watered, obscuring her view. She could hear the crack of wood intermittently punctuated with the steel striking stone. Now and then, out of the wet murk of her tear-soaked sight, Holna saw the glint of sparks.

She whirled around, sheathed her sword and brought both her hands to her chest. Facing the plains, she fumed. Her anger felt robust enough to fill the entire world before her. She heard the steel of her sword striking the stone figure echo in her mind. The memory of those concussions churned her feelings. She could smell blood, taste sweat and feel the exertion of so many years of combat in her body. The blanket was still draped over her but she did not feel it.

There was a soft sound off to Holna's left. She turned and drew her sword. It was the young hermit; he stood at the edge of the path that lead out of the woods. He looked at her as though he were made out of stone. Holna panted like a beast.

They remained motionless, focusing on one another as a breeze passed over them.

"Who are you?" Holna shouted.

The young hermit said nothing. He did not move.

"Who are you? Do you live here?" Holna said.

Again the young hermit said nothing and did not move.

"Why are you following me?" Her speech lightened as she recalled that she had also been following him.

The young hermit looked out to the plains. Then he looked at Holna and smiled. He gestured toward the plains as though he were inviting her to walk on. Holna said nothing.

The young hermit looked down at the path and strolled along it. He placed his hands behind his back as though he had not a care in the world. Holna kept her sword tip pointed at him as he ambled languidly over the stones; they crunched and shifted under his sandals. Only when he had stepped beyond the rock path and onto the grass did Holna sheath her sword. She waited until the young hermit was further out on to the plains, then she made her way along the path.

"Very well, I will call you Ulh," Holna said to herself and she drew the blanket around her arms.

A gust of wind and it wailed.

10.

A disembodied call from the woods.

Holna heard the bird's sharp and sweet song as she listened to her feet moving through the grass. The shift from the stone path to the grass had been a brief and dramatic change from the world of the forest to the plains. The path had sounded heavy and rough with the crunch of small stones, now the grass under each step was a light sweep and matched the openness of the sky and the plains. The open sky was at once soothing and unsettling, giving her more air in her lungs but also reminding her of her solitary voyage on the sea.

Ahead of Holna, Ulh walked carelessly with his hands behind his back. Not far beyond the path, the grass inclined steadily rising to the sky. As Ulh was ahead of Holna, he came to the ascent of the land first. Holna felt uneasy as to what was beyond the rise of the land. She slowed her pace.

Holna watched Ulh approach the ascent of the plains. Suddenly he bolted and ran up the hill vigorously pumping his arms. He zigzagged and then turned. His face was aglow as he looked back at Holna and then he continued up the hill.

As Ulh came to the top of the hill, he pushed himself even harder, as though he were in some race. He crested the slope and then disappeared. Holna stopped and looked to the right and to the left. The plains opened out to featureless horizons. "Follow Tor," she heard the head monk's voice, "without exception." She would never have crossed the sea otherwise; "Please, for me."

Holna continued on and cautiously made her way up the hill. She was at a total disadvantage facing uphill with Tor's light in her eyes and having no idea what was at the top. The only true indicator of her course was Tor, and at this very moment, it was guiding her to a vulnerable position, again.

When she was close to the top, Holna drew her sword hiding it at arm's length just behind her leg. Coming over the crest she could see the distant peaks of a mountain range. Then as the land leveled she saw Ulh sitting on the grass directly in line with Tor's progression. Before Ulh was a large crater. He sat at its edge. Drawing closer, Holna could see how the grass continued into the crater and that its bottom was filled with water. She stopped within two great steps between her and Ulh.

The water in the crater was dirty and the reflection of the cloud cover made the surface of the water a particular shade of grey-brown. Its colour and circular shape reminded Holna of the large gong in the centre of the temple.

She recalled how the gong would be struck in the morning and the evening. She remembered the sound of the monks' silent walks throughout the courtyard: their bare feet upon stone and the edges of their robes brushing the walkway.

Holna sheathed her sword. Ulh showed no notice of her.

Ulh, Tor and the crater were in direct alignment. Holna knew there would be no going around as the crater was very wide. Ulh sprang to his feet and looked back at Holna. She jumped back gripping the handle of her sword. Ulh smiled and then his face became very serious as he started to walk the perimeter of the crater. He looked down at his feet very intently as he placed each foot with great care.

Holna watched him to see where he was going. He continued along the edge of the crater, moving at a steady and vibrant pace. When Ulh was opposite Holna on the crater's other side, Holna approached the edge of the crater.

Holna looked into the silty waters and was amazed by how much it looked like the gong of the monastery. If she were to follow the headmonk's instructions, she must cross the water. *What difference would it make if I walked around it? It would not take long, I could run.* Then she remembered what happened the first day of her journey when she intentionally did not follow Tor.

When the monastery had been attacked, Holna had eluded their attackers in the encircling forest. She was filled with such anger that she ran until she was exhausted. In the morning, she had come to the shore of the sea and found a small moored boat. She did not want to cross the sea. She had never been in a boat and she could not swim. The head monk had said, "Walk with Tor," but the sea was in the direction of Tor's path. She must cross the sea to follow the head monk's directions, to follow his request, "for me."

She was very tired and even though it seemed she had evaded the attackers, she did not want to risk lingering at the shore too long. She did not know what to do. *Should I cross the sea or return home?* she had wondered. She felt within the fold of her top for what the head monk had given her. She took it out and looked at it. "For me," the head monk's voice sounded clearly in her mind and echoed in her heart.

She put it back within the fold of her top and went to the boat. She anxiously untied the rope fastened to the rock outcropping. She looked out to the sea. The air smelled of life and death; the waters moved slowly. She put the headmonk's request in the bottom of the boat. She stepped into the boat and it moved from side to side, the bottom striking the rocks beneath like so many knocking fists. The movement sent a current of fear through her.

This is nonsense, Holna thought. She threw the rope into the boat and stormed off. She walked opposite Tor's path and began to leave the shore. The boat floated out and away. When she was about to enter the woods in a direct line for her mountain home, she realized what the head monk had given her was not with her. Her heart ached with guilt and she remembered the head monk touching her heart centre. She searched her body frantically then the ground around her. She looked back along the path she had taken from the shore; what the head monk had entrusted her with was nowhere to be seen.

Holna ran to the boat; it had already begun to move out into the calm waters. She ran into the sea. She reached the boat; the water was up to her waist. In the bow was the head monk's request. She stood there for a moment feeling the pull of the sea's currents. The movements were forcing her to keep her balance and stay upright. "For me," came into her mind then filled her body. She climbed into the boat.

The memory of that moment burned in Holna's heart as she looked upon the murky waters in the crater. She let the memory go but an ache resonated a little longer in her heart.

Looking up at the crater, Holna could see that Ulh was now a quarter of the edge away from returning to where she stood. She stepped back from the crater's edge and placed her hand casually on the hilt of her sword. Ulh approached her and passed without changing his focused attention on his steps. He proceeded on to make another round of the crater.

As he continued along, Holna stepped onto the edge of the crater. She looked down at the waters. It could be deep or shallow.

She looked up at Tor and confirmed the alignment with her course, then slowly moved down the edge of the crater. She did not want the blanket to get wet or dirty so she took it off her back and threw it over her left shoulder. She walked carefully but the inclination forced her to lean back on one hand so that she would not fall into the water. As she came to the edge of the water, Holna could see how the grass went into the silt but she could not tell how far. She guessed that it was rainwater and that perhaps the bottom was grassy and bowled.

She sat on the grass of the crater's side. Ulh came around to her right along the crater's edge. As usual, he seemed to pay no notice of her.

She dipped the tip of her foot into the water and could feel a firm bottom. From the edge it seemed the water was very shallow. She reached out further with her foot and found level, solid ground. Holna stood at the water's edge.

Ulh now made his way along the edge to her left. Still he looked down watching his footsteps with great care. Holna stepped into the water and her foot met what felt like a hard bottom. She stepped into the water which was only as deep as her toes. When she was satisfied that the ground would support her, she lifted her other foot and held it over the surface of the water. Carefully, she placed the point of her foot beyond the water's surface and then settled it on the firm bottom beneath.

She stood there for a moment and waited. Then she bounced her weight on the bottom. It seemed secure. She began taking one step after another, deliberately checking the next step before taking another. She carried on with careful placement of each foot. As she progressed she felt more assured of the soundness of the base of the crater.

When Holna reached the centre of the crater, she paused to see where Ulh was. He was behind her and still walking the crater's edge. She looked up at Tor; a clear circle in its obscured position behind the thin smooth clouds that covered the sky.

Looking down at the water and being surrounded by that grey-brown colouring, Holna thought of the gong and heard it as she watched the ripples in the water emerge from the minute fluctuations of her feet.

She thought about the courtyard where the gong was kept. She recalled the faces of the child monks and the flowers that grew around the dormitory. The gong continued to sound within her as she took another step and remembered the food she ate with the monks and the ease with which they lived their lives. And yet, they hid behind walls.

Holna pulled out of her reverie. Her feet were cold and she decided to move quicker to finish the crossing. With a quicker and lighter gait she moved on but still remained mindful of ensuring a firm footing.

As Holna neared the edge of the water in the crater, Ulh approached from her left, watching each step he took. Holna's final step brought the toes of her front foot to the edge of the water. Ulh had stopped directly in front of her and blocked Tor. He still looked down at his feet. Holna watched him. Tor cast Ulh as a frozen silhouette.

Then Ulh titled his head a little as though he heard something on the horizon; Tor's light beamed from one side of his head and blinded Holna. He began to slowly lift his hand as though he were going to bring it to his face or say something. Holna moved her right hand closer to her sword and shaded her eyes with her left. Ulh's mood was inscrutable and Holna was again at the downgrade of an inclination of land with bright light in her eyes; she was vulnerable.

Ulh paused in his movement holding his right hand up. He seemed pensive or as though he were about to speak. Then he quickly threw out his hands at Holna and held them motionless with his palms splayed wide. He stayed in that position like a statue with both his arms extended towards her. When it seemed to Holna that Ulh was going to move no further, she relaxed her grip on her sword.

There was a crack and the crater collapsed under Holna; she threw out the blanket with her left hand and Ulh grabbed it. The weight and force of Holna's fall drew Ulh forward and he fell onto the sloping edge of the crater.

Holna held fast to the blanket with one hand and then grabbed on with the other. There was an immense sound of collapse and sucking beneath her. She fell against the side of the crater then clambered up the blanket as Ulh, now lying over the crater's edge and partially down its side, held the edge of the blanket tightly in both hands. Holna pounced right over him when she reached his hands. Ulh's wiry frame supported her as he still lay on the the edge of the crater which was now a bottomless chasm.

Ulh crawled away from the hole to Holna's side. She was panting and gripping the grass. Holna worked hard to keep in all she was feeling: the anger, the fear and her heartache. Holna violently took the blanket from Ulh with one hand while her other hand still clutched at the grass.

Holna looked at Ulh. He too was panting as he looked to where the crater had been. Then Ulh looked at Holna; there was an excitement in his eyes. Holna let go of her hold on the grass, stood and looked at the hole that only moments ago was a firm and shallow basin of water. She approached it cautiously. All that was left of the crater was a smooth-edged hole into a dark chasm. The edges were wet earth with a pungent aroma so strong that Holna could taste it.

From its depths they could hear the sounds of water, earth and stone. They were moving and gurgling like the final breaths of some giant animal dying and then they ceased.

An abrupt and formidable silence came from the chasm.

11.

The wind blew over the grass.

Holna and Ulh sat silently on the edge of the crater looking into the formidable aperture. Holna stern and stonefaced, Ulh smiling and peering enthusiastically into the newly formed abyss. Holna clung to the blanket with both hands. The fibres pressed into the lines of the skin on her fingers. How did he know the crater was going to sink? Why else would he have reached out to me? He must have known.

Holna turned to Ulh and said, "How did you know?"

Ulh looked at the opening.

"Hey!...You!" Holna raised her voice and then reached over and gave Ulh a push. He turned to her with a look of surprise.

"How...did...you...know?" Ulh looked at her cocking his head to one side, seemingly in thought and then turned around as though he had heard something.

"Ulh!" Holna yelled at him and shook him by the shoulder. He paid no attention to her. Then Ulh rose and examined the grass as he meandered towards the mountains.

Holna laid back in the grass. She looked at Tor directly above her. She forced her eyes open to the intensity of the light. When will you turn to stone? She heard the head monk's voice, "Please, for me."

She shut her eyes tight and felt tears stream slowly drown her cheeks. How long will this go on? When will you turn to stone?

Holna brought both her hands to the centre of her chest. She could feel the outline of what she carried, and beneath it, her heart aching with the memory of the head monk's touch. Tor's light was warm and gradually it soothed her. Holna felt herself sinking into the grass. When will you turn to stone? She felt herself sinking beneath the grass and to the ground beneath it. When will you turn to stone?

Even though the sun was on her face, she was far beneath the grass and deeply embedded in the ground; all was dark. She was of the soil, deeply set, cool and calm. She supported everything above; she allowed roots to move through her and she cradled the rivers and seas; she was the greater base to mountains and that which the sky hung over. She was the horizon from which Tor rose and set.

This is not possible, she thought, and sat up in a panic. She was now on the grass; she had arms, legs, hands and feet. Tor had moved dramatically and she had to crane back her neck to see it. Her experience had lasted for some time.

Holna looked down at the blanket in her hands and gripped it tightly as she waited for her heart to stop racing and her breathing to subside. Then she wrapped the blanket over her shoulders, stood and saw Ulh far ahead. He was moving around in semicircles and appeared to be looking for something in the grass. His path, indirect as it was, moved along in Tor's direction.

Holna looked back at the chasm in the ground which was once the firm base of the crater she had walked across. Her shadow lengthened into its dark depths. She turned and walked directly towards Tor.

Soft punctuations of grass plodded on.

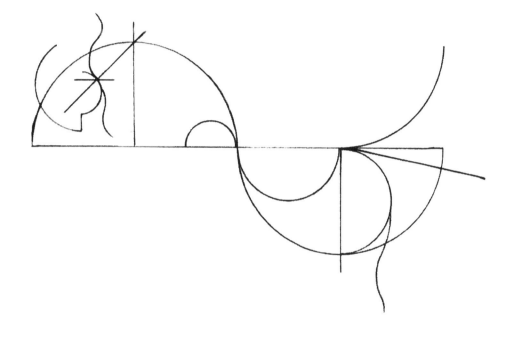

12.

A hard muted pulse insisted itself.

The scarring knife and the ink container knocked into one another in Holna's pack. The continuously uneven rhythm aggravated her. She took the blanket from her shoulders and then spread it on to the grass. She knelt and removed her pack. She placed the venison between the scarring knife and the ink container. Then she got to her feet, put on her pack, and walked on, dragging the blanket off the grass and throwing it over her shoulders once more.

Holna was far behind Ulh. She walked a direct line with Tor's descent. Ulh turning and crouching, traced irregular circular patterns upon the same line. Holna had walked wrapped in the blanket, listening to the sounds of her footfalls on the grass and the gentle movements of the wind as she watched the approaching mountain range. Now and then she would hear a subtle grunt from Ulh but nothing more.

It would soon be night and Holna was weary with the days walk in the open air of the plains. She was looking forward to nightfall and sleep. There were no trees or shelter, only vast swaths of grass and above islands of passing clouds. Far ahead, Tor gradually sank into the mountain range.

By nightfall they would still be on the plains. And so, with no nearby trees, there would be no fire for the night.

Holna stopped walking, removed her pack and sword, setting them aside. This is where I sleep tonight. She sat and watched Tor nestle between two mountain peeks. Its light shifted in its brilliance as it haloed passing clouds, deepening their whites and revealing shades of grey. The features of the mountains softened into dark silhouettes and became featureless masses. As Tor met the edges of the mountain silhouettes, its light became sharper and stronger. Holna wondered if this were its last setting, giving all that remained of its light and would not appear again on the other side of the world. Is this Tor turning to stone?

As Tor sank beyond the mountains, its light became yellows and oranges that bled into reds. As it disappeared, the clouds were lit in a kaleidoscope of the same yellows and oranges, briefly became a blood red and then Tor was gone. The clouds were white again and the blue of the sky darkened.

Holna reclined into the grass and wrapped the blanket around her. Points of light appeared one at a time until the black of the sky was full with its usual host of stars.

"Walk with Tor, follow its path without exception," the head monk's voice was soft. Holna heard and felt his words. They echoed inside her and then she spoke them, "Follow its path without exception."

Again she said them to the sky. The words reached the stars and filled the areas of black between them. As she continued to speak she changed her enunciation so that a certain word was fully voiced and the others whispered:

"Follow…its path without exception."

"Follow…its path…without exception."

"Follow its path…without…exception."

"Follow its path without…exception."

She continued to rotate the phrase with this progression, speaking to the stars and the dark. With every full-voiced utterance was a great extension of herself, not only into the sky, but out concentrically from her to the great expanse of the plains. Like a stone dropped in water, her words rippled outwards in expanding circles and gentle waves over the surface of the ground and out among the stars. She was moving the world around her.

Holna continued speaking skyward and feeling the undulating effects on the grass until she felt sleepy. When she stopped speaking out loud, the silence was as a deep infinite pause. As though she had posed a question and the replier, somewhere among the stars and the grass, was pondering their response. Why with so many stars do my eyes never hurt or water as when I look upon Tor? It is but one, they are many. She fell asleep.

> Holna looks into her cupped hands.
> A point of light within,
> floating,
> shining.
> The light is cool, no heat.
>
> There is a sound, from within the light,
> it beats and quakes against Holna's palms,
> her fingers.
> Her skin trembles.
> The sound grows,
> the light is opening,
> the sound deepens,
> the light is opening.
>
> It becomes infinite points of light,

they are singing,
they are crying,
they are laughing.

The lights seep into Holna's hands.
A singing,
a crying,
a laughing.

"Who is it?" she asks, embraced in the dark,
"Who is it for?"
"What is it for?"
"Why is it?"
The silent embracing dark.

"Why?"

Holna walks.
She is young,
she is a child.
Her hair hangs in her face, she looks down at her bare feet,
the soil of a forest.
She sees her hand in the head monk's hand.
They walk among trees, the trees sing, she can smell their songs.

They stop walking.
The head monk gently taps Holna between the eyes,
the trees sing louder.
He taps again,
the soil sings.

He taps again;
he laughs, Holna laughs.

All is laughter.

13.

A deep rhythmic breath.

Holna looked down at her feet and listened to her steps in the grass. She looked up and saw Ulh examining the grass like a hunting dog, sniffing the ground, hunched over, at times on all fours.

When Holna had awoken, Tor had just breached the horizon, displaying the smooth contour of the plains. Ulh was nowhere to be seen. She had eaten some venison and then aligned herself with Tor's ascent and continued her journey. She watched the shadows over the plains recede with the morning's daylight. Where do shadows go? she wondered, just as Ulh leapt up from out of the grass and the last of shadows in between the blades. Holna had never thought about shadows before. Her entire journey had been full of new considerations and questions. These unknown places had brought new experiences within herself. She recalled the chain of events: the attack on the monastery, the boat across the sea, the beach, the forest and the stone in the clearing, the house, the plains and finally the crater. How did Ulh know that it was going to collapse?

The sound of Holna's feet moving through the grass was equally unsettling and comforting. On the one hand, every step reminded her of the crater opening beneath her even when it had seemed so stable, while the sound of the grass beneath her feet was so soothing. The contradiction reminded her of the sea.

Often during her voyage she would find herself calmed by the lapping of the waves on the side of the boat. Sometimes she would stop rowing to watch the waves and peer within their movements. The sea had invisible depths and it teamed with all sorts of known and unknown life. It was at once unsettling and comforting. The similarity between the plains and the sea made Holna feel that they were the same. Just as the sea, the plains, as barren as they appeared, were full of active life.

Imagining the plains as the sea, Holna believed she could hear water. It was thin and light within the swish of her steps in the grass. The liquid sound grew and suddenly there was a stream before her. It ran from north to south. It was shallow but had a strong current. She went on all fours and cupped the water. It was very cold. She sipped at it and its temperature stung her teeth and lips.

She looked up and saw Ulh pulling something out of the ground. He fell back and held a brownish object in his hands. He looked around for Holna, spotting her at the stream, he rushed to her and sat on the opposite bank. He held out what he had in his hands and smiled; they were roots.

Ulh washed them in the stream with great excitement. Then he broke one of them in half. He beamed at what he saw and showed it to Holna. The flesh inside was purple. Ulh smelled it, touched the flesh with the tip of his tongue and swirled the flavour in his mouth. Again he smiled, took a great big bite and chewed voraciously.

As Ulh continued to eat ravenously, Holna sat down, removed her pack and took out some venison. She ate slowly as she watched the movement of the water in the stream. She focused on the reflection of Tor in the currents. She watched how the round brilliance of Tor was broken up and its light was lengthened by the moving water.

From where she sat, Holna could also see Ulh's reflection in the water. His features were silhouetted, and like Tor's reflection, was distorted by the stream's currents. Ulh's silhouette was shifted into tiny fragments or lengthened in the flow of water. Both Tor and Ulh's silhouette retained some of their original form, but only because Holna knew it apart from the disfiguring reflections.

"For me." Holna heard the head monk's voice. She realized "me" was a reflection in her mind and there was a clear form of "me" that she could not grasp. Feeling the words in her heart deepened her understanding: the sensation in her chest and the words in her mind were like the reflection of Tor in the stream.

Ulh had finished his root feast and went to the edge of the stream, splashing water into his mouth. Ulh's actions added to the disruption of reflections in the stream. Holna watched as the currents and movements returned to their original flow, still distorting and shifting the reflection of Tor within the natural dynamics of the stream. I can see Tor but I cannot touch it. I need it but I do not know what it is. I can touch the water, I can drink the water, but Tor is not in it. Is it?

The light began to soften. Looking up, Holna saw thick, dark grey clouds rolling in over Tor. She looked at Ulh. "Let us continue," she said, and pointed at the clouds. Ulh smiled back at her and began walking towards Tor.

Tor was a soft impression within the clouds. It was easy to look upon. Holna wondered why the clouds do not move around Tor as the smoke from a fire passes around trees and other objects. "Walk with Tor, follow its path without exception until it turns to stone." Again Holna heard the head monk's voice. What does that mean? Is that like a fire, when the wood burns and you are left with the remains, the embers? Does that mean Tor is going to go out? Am I following the end of Tor, the end of the world?

Holna brought her hands to her chest and felt what she carried. The edge of it was hard and the mystery of it was in keeping with the head monk's words and the sound of his voice. She had tied his request over heart as though to harbour his words. She had never felt such perplexing feelings from so little: a touch, a few words and such a small object. "Me!" boomed throughout her mind and her body.

Her whole journey was so confusing and yet so simple. Every day she followed Tor as it moved through the sky. Yet following Tor with its assured rise and path had lead Holna to unknown places. She was continually moving towards an unknown destination that would only be shown when her guide, Tor, changed in an impossible way. How can Tor become stone?

Holna watched Ulh as he rolled over and over again in the grass. He moved quickly and he was so agile but his direction was always so erratic. He moved well and he used his whole body but Holna doubted he had any concern about where he was going. He continually stayed with Tor's path, another mystery with all the others. Within the pace of her steps, Holna kicked at the grass and remembered the sea.

A single accent that softened into a regular breath.

14.

Rain in the dark.

Holna woke to a bitter cold and she was wet. When night had come, Holna had fallen asleep on the plains in the warm curl of the blanket, now it was gone. She looked for it in the dark finding only soaked grass. She reached out further and further seeking it. A hand touched her shoulder, she knocked it away and grabbed the handle of her sword.

"Ulh, I have lost the blanket! It is gone!" Holna shouted. She could still feel its warmth and recalled the dim presence of Tor at dusk behind the clouds as it nestled over the mountain range. She had lain on her side, her pack under her head as Tor's light had diminished. She longed for that deepening warmth within the blanket.

Ulh grabbed Holna by the elbow and pulled her up. He picked up her pack, strapped it to her back, then they were off. Ulh pulled Holna on through the dark and the rain.

"We cannot go yet. Tor is not here, it has not risen," she cried. Ulh said nothing, only breathed heavily as he continued to guide her along by the elbow in the rain.

Without the blanket, Holna felt so exposed. The rain was a stinging cold, the wet grass made walking difficult. Holna felt a numbness within dragging her down and encroaching on her will to continue. Ulh pulled her along as she cared less and less about where they were going. She brought her hands to her chest and felt the outline of what she carried, "for me" she heard the head monk's voice.

Holna's head spun. She wanted to feel the blanket in her hands, she wanted it wrapped around her. She remembered the house in the woods. She could smell the fire and feel its heat. She wanted to stop, to build a home, somewhere, in any wood away from all that she had ever known. She wanted to stop looking for answers. She wanted all questioning to stop, no more guidance from Tor and no more mysteries. Holna fell to the ground.

Ulh pulled at Holna's arm. "No, Tor is not in the sky." she said, refusing to go on.

Ulh grabbed both of her arms trying to pull her up to her feet. He let her go and she fell on her back. The cold rain pounded her face; Holna was soaked. I should have let the sea take me or the sink hole in the crater.

She was retreating within herself. She heard the head monk's voice, "Me." It sounded different. The scale of it and what was within it was growing. "Me" was becoming a maelstrom of a multitude of places and spaces within her; it was all her emotions, all her thoughts, it was every way she had ever moved her body all culminated together. As this maelstrom grew, the cold sharp concussions of the rain continued to strike her face.

"Me."

The question of it, the nature of it, and the reason for it were becoming too much. She was coming apart. All sensation was a blurred force expanding within her. The rain continued pounding on her face as she lay in the grass.

"Me" echoed through Holna's mind, her heart and her body.

Holna wanted an end to all that she was experiencing. She wanted death and was no longer concerned for her scars. She had never felt this way. She had always wanted to be before the gods having fulfilled all the great scarrings meant for her and made by her. But now she wanted to succumb to a scar that was different, a scar that ended her life, not the scars that formed her life. Her tribe believed the world came of a scar, it was the first great opening of the original dark that let light in. All nature was the intricacy of this original scarring. Ripples in the water, the bark of trees, skin, the air moving through the sky, all were scarrings. Life marking itself to sustain life, not to undo it.

Each drop of rain came, one after the other, as a continuity with no variation until Holna felt a new physical force. The rain began to include a harder strike among all the drops. The sting of it dwindled and the desire to die returned. Another strike, then another. The desire for death moved back. The impacts were as a focused weight of the rain coming together for one concussive moment upon her. The desire to die was gone and the darkness of the plains and the rain came fully into her awareness. Suddenly the remaining maelstrom of emotions and sensations left completely as she felt a hard slap on her face.

Holna began to cry. This was something she had not done since she was young. It was difficult for her to cry and now it was the only thing she could do as the rain fell on her. The sensation was throughout her body and it sickened her. This is weakness, she thought.

Holna sobbed and pushed down a deeper release that she believed she could not survive. Then she felt a hand wiping away her tears. In the dark of the great space of the plains, in the invisible working of the world, a silent hand alleviated her of her tears and brushed them among all the bitterly cold rain drops. There was a warmth - she felt it was in the distant sound of her crying and the hand clearing her face of her tears - they were somehow related.

Holna's crying subsided but it lay deep inside her unfinished. Ulh gently lifted her as she held on to his shoulder and pushed up with her legs; she helped him to help her. They walked on.

The grass sounded the relenting assault of the rain. Their footsteps were wet punctuations within the torrent. Holna imagined they were walking in water and then there was a flash of lightning. The sharp burst revealed the plains. The experience brought Holna out of her emotional numbness and her pace began to match Ulh's. Thunder sounded and it was so close that it shook Holna from within as though the world was cracking open. Just as the sound moved through the plains, it moved within her, reaching unknown places and spaces. She felt the thunder had access to her in ways she did not know.

Another flash of light. Holna brought her hands over her heart and braced for the thunder. It could go where the light could not. The thunder sounded again and it was closer this time, directly above them. It struck even harder within Holna. She tensed up and forced down the need to cry. It was an injury to resist. She did not want to hear herself cry again. But it was as though the world wanted her to cry. This was the scar she did not want. She did not want to give into it, she did not want to be vulnerable to what she would see of herself.

Holna looked for a distraction. She brought her hands away from her chest and what she carried and grabbed the handle of her sword. It did nothing to alleviate the feeling. She dug her nails into left forearm, she was sure she broke the skin, still the desire to cry lingered.

Again there was a flash of light. Holna saw the mountain range, thunder came and Holna stumbled. Ulh held her up by the elbow. Seeing the range flash in and out of sight brought Holna back to her journey. They could find their way to the mountain range, leave the plains and escape this painful vulnerability.

Holna hardened her resolve and looked towards the mountain range in the dark. "More lightning, more lightning," she pleaded.

Another sliver of light, a great spark that opened the dark. Holna's pace was now surpassing Ulh's and he let go of her elbow. She hurried ahead of him and readied herself for the thunder. I will not let it in. Tor has come in the night to show me the way. It has scarred the dark.

The thunder was silenced.

15.

The rain was a soft hiss.

In the deep dark of the plains, Holna walked quickly. There was no sign of Ulh. Holna had felt and heard him close by until all she heard was the rain. She knew that the range of mountains was not far. As she walked on, Holna could hear the change in timbre of the rainfall. Within the uniform din of the rain hitting the grass of the plains came a higher frequency. Moving closer she could discern the sounds of rain hitting foliage. The woods of the mountain were just before her.

With each step Holna felt the land change. The grass thinned and the ground became harder. The sound of her footsteps were freed of the sloshing of wet grass as they became more distinct punctuations: it was the evolving pulse of her step within the drone of the rain. She walked until the rain no longer fell on her and she could feel the closeness of trees. Holna could not hear any indication of Ulh.

"Ho! Are you here!?" she called out. There was no reply.

Holna stood in the dark listening for Ulh. She was filled with the void of an unanswered call while the rain continued to sound high above in the shelter of the unseen trees. Standing before an invisible mountain with its silent looming presence became all too much for her. The void of no response grew in Holna, it made the cold on her skin intensify and creep into her bones. Everything that had brought her there, every choice she had made and every event that was out of her control, coursed into her bones and made her feel a cold she had never known.

She withdrew inside herself and everything around her receded. What she felt of the world, the air, the land, the smells and sounds, all began to move away. She saw the great hole in the ground where the water had been, where she had felt a firm ground beneath her, where she had heard the gong sound so peaceful within her mind, all of that had been consumed into an abyss. She had difficulty breathing. She felt a fear, a terror, that she could not name or identify growing within her. Gradually it began to radiate outwards beyond her. On the plains she had contemplated ending her life, now there was something within her seeming to operate of its own volition. She did not want what was happening but it was overtaking her. What is doing this? I am sinking, falling into a hole, a blackness. Are these the scars of the world, of the gods?

There was movement close by. She could do nothing but notice it as the terror within her and the distancing of the world continued. Then there was a burst of flame and there was a fire.

Ulh squatted close to it. His smiling face glowed into view. All Holna's sensations of withdrawing paused, and in a sliver of time there were two experiences of the world: one distant and unhinged from her, the other a warmth drawing near.

Ulh gestured to her to come to the fire. He added more wood to the flames. Holna walked over to the fire slowly with deliberate steps as though she had never seen fire before. Each step felt as an uncertain ground beneath her, and she felt so fragile that she would shatter. It took great will for her to move to the fire, but as she did, in subtle increments, the world came closer. She looked at Ulh, his face was alight with happiness and as always there was that mischievousness in his eyes. Holna slowly squatted by the fire. The heat and light was a sublime antithesis to what she had just experienced and it reached her where the wet and cold could not. She remembered the head monk touching her in the centre of her chest.

Looking around, Holna could see rock formations leading to the sharp ascent of the mountain. Opposite, the trees opened onto the deep dark of the plains. The trees were sparsely placed, tall with thick trunks. The ground was hard and dotted with medium-sized stones.

Ulh reached for a couple of nearby stones and began creating a ring around the fire. He rose and left coming back with another stone. Holna watched him leave and come back. He did this a number of times with great care until the fire was completely encircled.

Ulh sat in front of the fire opposite Holna. She was struck with the comfort and intimacy she felt. The way the fire roared, the contour of the black stones, the trees above sounding the drone of the falling rain, Ulh sitting before her, they all culminated into a softening and a yielding from within her. This deepening comfort scared Holna; she stood up quickly as though to leave but managed to keep from walking away.

Out on the plains she had been overcome with a receding inwards that drew her away from the world, now there was a rushing outwards from within her towards the world. Her fear grew as the desire to experience the intimacy and comfort called to her. Holna could not hold back any longer, she fell to her knees, covered her face with her hands and began to cry.

She felt that her whole body, her mind and her heart were convulsing towards her end; that this is how she would die, crying. She could make no sense of how she felt or thought, all sensation was mixed and confused, it was an uncontrolled release. The sound of her own crying revolted her and yet she could do nothing but let it come out. Holna cried until her face and hands were soaking wet, far beyond what the rain had done. The experience left her fatigued.   In the light of the fire, on her knees, Holna wiped away her tears. She felt a fullness of being open, and with it, so too the world was larger. Everything including her was a continual expansion. She looked up to see Ulh smiling at her. His expression was of such a profound knowing that Holna felt as though he knew everything that she had been through in the entirety of her life. There was nothing keeping him from knowing her and yet she thought him the most profound enigma.

Ulh stood and went to a small nearby tree with low lying branches. He turned his back to Holna and took off his robe and placed it on one of the branches. In the dim fluctuations of firelight, Holna could see many scars on his back. His thin and frail frame carried deep wounds. He had been whipped repeatedly, more than once, as there were layered hatchings, a history of crossings and gouges. The firelight and its creation of shadow made his back look as an old landscape, like a scarred and bleak wasteland made over thousands of years. She marvelled at how he could have endured what looked to be such painful experiences. And yet, when he turned around, his face and his eyes were full of life, vigour and joy that she could not believe.

Ulh stood naked in front of Holna. He did not shiver or show any repulsion or discomfort to the cold. Nothing affects him. I do not understand him at all.

Ulh sat across from Holna. They looked into the flames. The roar and crackle echoed throughout the surrounding trees and the rain continued; one force rising, another falling. In the diametric opposition of the fire's heat and the cold air of the night, Holna thought of the blanket. She wanted it, she needed it. Her wet leather tunic clung to her body and deepened the chill. She put her hands up to the fire to warm them. The firelight and the shadows it cast on her hands made her skin look older and thicker than the worn leather of her tunic that came around her thumb. Her gaze followed the length of leather along her left sleeve and rested on the freshly scarred area beneath. What am I living for?

Holna stood and began to remove her garments. She started at her neck. As she shed her clothes, Ulh saw the extensive markings on her body. She was sinuous and athletic. There were figures of creatures and other shapes that he did not understand. They all linked together, some were faded. On her left arm was scarring that continued out from the ink, it was red and inflamed. He could see that she had never had children.

Holna placed her clothes on a nearby branch. Then she returned to the fire and stood in front of Ulh, only her chest covered with a length of cloth. It was wrapped and within it, Ulh could see the edges of a small square object. Holna untied the cloth at her back and carefully let the cloth and the object fall into her hands. She held it very carefully and looked at it for a moment. She knelt in front of the fire opposite Ulh.

Holna took a deep breath and then unwrapped the cloth. Inside was a waxy object. It was square shaped and about a thumbs diameter in thickness. Holna held it up to Ulh. From the firelight, Ulh could see that it was a book completely sealed in wax. He could make out a pattern beneath the wax, it was a symbol inlaid on the cover of the book.

Ulh jumped with joy and gesticulated as though he was having an attack or trying to free something from within himself. He carried on, jumping and throwing his arms around.

When some degree of composure came to him, he sat back down in front of the fire but he was still giddy and excited. Beaming with joy he looked at Holna. Then he became very pensive as though he were trying to figure something out.

"How did I get it?" Holna asked.

Ulh nodded.

"It was given to me by a…it was his…" she paused and then corrected herself, "…it was given to me as a dying wish."

Ulh smiled at Holna and then jiggled his shoulders as though he were dancing on the inside.

"Do you know what this means?" Holna asked.

Ulh nodded with a smirk.

"Tell me!" Holna pleaded as she shook the book.

Ulh looked away, rubbing his head.

"Tell me!" Holna shouted, sitting forward. "Tell me! I have been carrying this…" looking at the book made her heart ache, "…this book and…"

Ulh clapped his hands together, it thundered out beyond the trees and into the falling rain. The sound startled Holna out of her mind's burdens and her heart's frustrations. Ulh's face was as stone. He kept his hands together, palm to palm and placed them against his forehead. It reminded Holna of a gesture the monks made in greeting. Then Ulh rubbed his palms together as he lowered them. The sound they made was a smooth oscillation like a rolling and receding tide. Holna remembered the sea and the loneliness she felt on the water.

Ulh's expression became stern. Holna saw in his eyes a distance as though he had left for a moment. Then Ulh lowered his head and took a deep breath. He made a quiet growling sound at the back of his throat as he exhaled. He looked at Holna with deep eyes, a depth she had never seen before. He drew her in and reached out to her. She felt uneasy and did not know what to do. She had never felt this kind of vulnerability.

Ulh leaned onto his hands and knees; he looked like some animal on all fours as his eyes opened from their contemplative weight to a mischievous width. He put his face just before the fire; Holna could see his features so clearly. Ulh opened his mouth and left it open. Holna thought he was going to speak, but he did not. Ulh opened his mouth a little wider and tilted his head forward slightly. The dark of his mouth was illuminated inside like a torch being brought into a cave; it was a chasm of misaligned teeth, moist skin, and no tongue. A severed stub, jaggedly cut, rested at the threshold of his throat in a silent unobstructed passage.

Holna jumped back and felt her chest open with a longing and an ache. She was overcome with a profound need to care for him and knew that there was no way to fulfill it. She put her hand to her mouth to cover a gasp as the other hand covered her heart. She looked at him with wide eyes, her mouth and heart covered. She recognized the sound she had made in the shock, it was something she had not done since she was a little girl.

Ulh closed his mouth. He sat back and looked upon Holna. The mischievousness receded and an age filled his eyes. Holna saw that it wasn't a fatigue, or wisdom, it was a will of patient journeying. An unknown voice sounded in Holna's mind, "There is more, always more."

Then the glint of mischievousness and joy came back into Ulh's eyes. He stood straight up and went over to the little tree and took his robe from the branch.

"Wait, what do I do? What do I do with this book?" Holna said.

Ulh shook out his robe, walked over to Holna and handed it to her. She took the robe and then Ulh pointed up at the mountain side as he smiled. He turned and left. She watched him go into the dark between the trees. As the light left his body, Holna saw the jagged formation of scars on his back. The entire landscape of his body was swallowed into the dark. She knew she would not see him again.

Alone at the fire, Holna examined the robe. It was dirty and stained but it had little aroma. She took a deep inhalation of it, the robe did not smell as bad as she thought it would. It smelled old and mildly pungent, yet it had a surprisingly deep warmth in its aroma. It was still damp so she returned the robe to the little tree to dry it out some more.

Holna crouched close to the fire, holding her knees. The book lay on a nearby stone. Light from the fire caught the faint silhouette of the symbol buried within the wax. She remembered the last moment she saw the head monk, he too was a silhouette. Beyond him was the meditation chamber and their attackers climbing the stairs. His shaded figure seemed so exposed in a place that she had come to know as calm and secure. The last time she was there it had been on the brink of being violated. Her mind played over what had happened when their attackers reached that room. Her heart ached. "Please, for me," she heard the head monk's voice and she pulled her legs closer to her chest. The cold within her began to appear. She stood up and put more wood on the fire.

Later, when she felt sleep coming, Holna took Ulh's robe, now dry and warm, and wrapped herself in it. She listened to the fire. The sound of flames and cracks with their amorphous and rapid movements ushered her into sleep.

>Holna stands,
>on the plains,
>in the dark.

>A pulse of light from the sky begins, it is a beat,
>an even continuity,
>a tap upon the shoulder.

>The plains are lit, and relit.
>With every flash something changes.

>A building.
>No building.
>More buildings.
>People walk about.
>So many roads of stone.
>Only grass.
>A great tower.

- Hax-Sus -

There are strange lights everywhere.
Mysterious buildings, so high, gleaming glass and metal.
Huge creatures, monsters, lumbering beasts, winged serpents.

No sound.
Darkness.

Then the slow growth of a single thunder strike.
The plains open.
Holna falls.

The low slow drag of a sounding thunder clap,
it becomes a scream
of thousands of voices.
Churning harmonies,
creating and annihilating,
pulse, rhythm,
smooth gestures, fractured meetings.

Without clarity,
of source or of purpose.

A distant echo.

16.

A gentle rustling of leaves at daybreak.

In the dawn's light, Ulh saw more detail in the unusual trees around him. There were no such trees in his forest dwelling. Everything was different in this place: the air, the forest, the grass and the sky.

Ulh was close to the base of the mountain. He came upon a community of large black stones. They were elongated with straight veined edges and coming out of the ground at different angles, most of them pointing skyward. He walked slowly among them, touching them as he moved from one to another. He had never seen stone quite like this. It was hard and brittle, sometimes pieces of the stone would come away and he would be holding flakes and shards. He felt an equivalent strength and vulnerability in the stones.

Ulh continued towards the mountain; he was coming close to the mountain's inclination where the stones converged and soon became a single mass merging with the mountain side. He heard a high pitched whistle rise and fall. Ulh stopped and waited. Moments later, he heard the same whistle. He moved towards it.

After clambering over some of the jagged outcroppings of stone within the large features of rock from the mountain, Ulh found a deep shaded area and within it was an opening into the mountain. It was like a gaping mouth of black stone: one darkness holding another.

Ulh knew this place, he had seen it. It would take him where he needed to go. He tempered his excitement as he approached the opening cautiously. He placed a hand on the edge of the black rock to steady himself as he looked into the dark of the cave. "Seek a great crossing, across and within the world," he remembered.

There was a single drop of water bisecting the opening. It fell at regular intervals. Ulh watched the drops and listened to the smack each drop made on the stone of the cave entrance.

"Pools, pools," he thought.

Each drop of water met the edge of the opening and trickled down a smooth slope that went into the cave. The descent was slick with moisture and reflected the outside light, illuminating the descent. Ulh considered sliding down the smooth cave floor but he could not see where the inclination lead. It may very well drop into a chasm or lead to a perilous grouping of sharp rocks. The safest option was to walk upright down the inclination as he braced himself within the narrow passage of the cave wall for support.

He stepped on to the cave entrance. He held firmly the surrounding rock and contemplated his next move. A drop of water tapped his crown. The sensation was cold and electrifying, it sent shivers through his body. Drink or drown, must cross, across and within the world, he thought.

The drops of water continued to tap the top of his head in a slow steady pulse. He revelled in the exhilaration of its temperature with its soothing rhythm.

Ulh knew he had found the correct entrance, the threshold into the mountain. He felt no rush to make the descent. He continued to feel the drops fall on him as he listened to the seam of sound: the dry non-reverberant space of the outside world behind him, and the reverberance that came from within the world of the mountain before him.

It was not until his head was quite soaked that he took his first step into the caves. His foot slipped and he immediately realized how much of his upper body would carry him down. Moving away from the drip of water was a move away from a support. Drink or drown, he thought.

Ulh inched his way down the inclined tunnel bracing his hands and setting his feet as firmly as he could. Every step felt as though he were going to slip, or that he would be violently pulled forward due to the slope of the entrance. The process was painful, it commanded so much of his muscles that it felt as though his bones ached. He had to keep his head down as he pushed out through his arms; it was the only way to ensure his footing.

As he continued with careful steps and strained muscles pushing outward against the cold stone, Ulh could hear the water dripping at the cave opening behind him. He found himself longing for that time when the water had dripped on his crown. The distracted thought caused him to lose his footing, he pushed hard into stone to support himself. He was overcome with the realization of how so much of the moment depended on his body and his actions braced against the stone wall of the mountain. Every movement he made and every thought was giving form and support to the entire mountain. He was directly responsible for the mountain's stability. The thought was at once empowering and ridiculous. He suppressed the urge to laugh, that it might cause him to lose his balance and fall down the slippery slope.

Ulh continued, inching his hands along the rough texture of the cave wall, creeping his feet over the slickness of the stone beneath him. He heard the echo of the dripping water at the entrance behind him. Each drop pounded into the space and drifted out before him. The pulsing echoes were a stark contrast to the rigidity of his limbs. The echoing drops moved freely, floating and swirling. As he carefully moved, thoughts of water swarmed his mind with images of the effect water had over time in this passage. He thought how one drop after the other had made this cave out of a long and slow rhythmic continuity. The thoughts and images were so palpable to him that he felt that time and that process within him; he felt that the great expanse of time that formed the opening accompanied him along his present journey. Again he suppressed the urge to laugh.

Ulh came to the end of the inclined portion of the entrance. Although it was still slick, the rock underfoot had leveled and now he could stand fully upright after being hunched over during his descent. Looking forward, his relative position to the opening obscured the light coming from the entrance and so his own shadow obscured what was beyond him. There was a void before him and he played a role in its formation. From his vantage point it was either solid rock or a drop of unknown depths.

The sound within the cave of the echoing drops at the opening gave him no accurate indication of the space before him. Pools, pools, he thought. My shadow deepens shadow, openings into openings. Pools, pools, drink or drown, must cross.

Ulh listened to the drops of water. His gaze fixed on the dark of his shadow, in a surround of dark stone, his limbs began to shake and ache to their very marrow. In the discomfort again came a need to laugh and the drops sounded fully into his awareness again. Taking in that sound and the support the drops had given him at the opening, he timed his step to leave the inclined rock and move out into the unknown before him just as a drop of water would sound. Drown or dink, he thought.

The sounds of dripping water moved freely into the dark before Ulh. He felt the rhythm and then he took a step down. It was a short step to solid rock. At first he felt a little foolish for thinking it may have been a deep chasm, then he looked back and up at the aperture. The light was blinding coming into such a dark place. It made sense to be confused by such clear opposites so close.

The distance Ulh had crossed into the cave was not very far, yet he was exhausted. He sat and looked up at the opening watching the drops of water continue to bisect the opening and reverberate into the cave.

Ulh listened to his breathing. It didn't fill the cave as the sounds of dripping water, but he could feel the size of it within himself. As his breathing relaxed and he rested, he knew the opening he came through was not the true opening he sought. He knew that aperture was somewhere in these caves. This opening was only the beginning, what he sought was a great chamber that opened to a great abyss. Pools, pools, he thought.

Ulh turned to the dark of the caves. He went down on all fours and slapped the stone floor with his hand. The sound reverberated out before him. He struck again and this time he began to hear more depth to the dark. Again he struck and more depth was revealed. He moved forward on all fours reaching into the dark to find his way.

Breaths and movements reverberated.

17.

The last of the burning embers hissed.

Holna stood at the circle of stones and the charcoal remnants of the night's fire. She had slept for a little while, but with first light she woke suddenly, as she was intent on beginning her climb of the mountain.

Holna took Ulh's robe from the little tree and placed it over her shoulder. She had laid the wax sealed book on a nearby stone. It was the first night since the head monk had given it to her that she had not slept with it tied to her chest. She picked up the book and took it out from its cloth wrapping. She looked at the symbol on the front. What did Ulh see? What does this mean?

She gently touched the wax over the symbol. She was filled with a desire to pry the wax off and open the book. How would I even know what it says, what it means? She heard the head monk's voice, "Me." She tensed and flinched. The sound of his voice went through her whole body. When the sensation had passed she looked down at the book. Her fingerprint was molded into the wax. The curves of her fingerprint crossed the lines of the embedded symbol, two images superimposed, distant and yet unified in the overlay.

Holna put the book back down on the stone and went to her pack. Sitting by the book, she opened her pack and took out the scarring knife, the ink container and the venison. She had enough to eat for another day; in a day or two she would need to hunt. That would be difficult if she needed to stay with Tor's direction throughout the sky.

Holna bit a portion of the venison and looked at the book. For the monks, reading and writing were so important, yet they spoke very little. Holna had always found it peculiar that it was more important for them to mark paper than their own bodies. The monks had no scars and they were so quiet. To Holna, they were like ghosts or shadows. They were in the world and not there.

Holna remembered the gong sounding in the courtyard. The memory of the sound was soothing and then she remembered the attack and seeing the young monks escorted into the courtyard surrounded by armed men. Anger grew in her heart. She pushed back the memory and put the remaining venison in her pack.

Holna began to wrap the book in the cloth and looking at the remains of the night's fire, she decided to hold the book during her climb. Scars should be seen. Holna resisted the urge to look at the inkless scars she had made on her arm.

She wrapped the scarring knife and ink container in the cloth. She put them in her pack along with Ulh's robe and strapped her sword to her waist.

Holna walked to the treeline at the edge of the plains. She watched Tor rising. She turned and found the alignment for her path up the mountain. She walked back into the woods and passed the remains of the fire. It was a circle of black stones and charred black wood; darkness encircling darkness. Holna touched the inkless scars beneath her leather sleeve. The slight sting of pain rose into the back of her neck. She grunted and walked beyond the embers.

The incline of the mountainside was steep, and appeared to have no change in the ascent; it was to be a long slow climb. There were many trees, so following Tor's direction would be a challenge. But if the grade of the ascent remained as steep as it was, she could use that as a partial guide. *As long as the walk is hard, then I know I am going in the right direction.*

She began her ascent with slow, even steps. The ground was hard for the most part and made the climb easy. The aroma of the trees was rich, unlike the plains which were a great expanse of fresh and odourless air. As she climbed, Holna kept a fixed gaze on the ground in front of her, turning now and again towards the sky when she came to an opening in the trees. She would wait to ensure she was in line with Tor's movement across the sky and then she would continue her climb.

Moving through the trees, the light began to change. When Holna reached another opening in the canopy, clouds had passed over Tor. They were not dense so she could still monitor its path but they soon brought snow. The flakes were small and it took some time before the snow stayed on the ground. At midday, Holna found a large tree where there was some ground free of snow and sat beneath it. She ate the last of the venison. She chewed slowly to savour every bite.

As she ate, Holna examined the symbol on the front of the small book and wondered at its meaning. She had seen similar markings in the monastery. She had seen the monk's writing and never asked what they meant. They were different from the marks and symbols on her body. Her markings were as animals or trees but these markings were very different. She regretted not asking what their writing meant or said. The symbol on the cover was so captivating. Its form was raised in the wax, Holna tilted the book trying to get more light and see within the wax. The symbol looked like it was made from metal or stone.

Again she pondered opening the book. I will not understand what is inside. Why force open something I cannot understand? It will not tell me why I am doing this, it will not tell me how Tor will turn to stone, and even if the answers were inside, I would not understand. She heard the head monk's voice, "Please, for me."

There was a momentary break in the clouds and rays of light came down on the mountainside. Illuminating the snow, the light looked cold and sent a chill through Holna. She had enough of contemplating the book. Having sat for some time, her body temperature had dropped. She stood, took Ulh's robe out of her pack and wrapped it around her head and shoulders. She continued up the mountainside.

Holna's journey up the mountain was slow, she stopped whenever there was sight of Tor beyond the trees so that she could maintain her alignment with it. The snow continued to fall. Then the ground started to level slightly but as the light of day was diminishing, she could not see clearly before her. There appeared to be an obscured outcropping. From its size, Holna concluded that it could only be a stone. As she approached it, the light diminished more and more. Holna was drawn to the dark mass. Moving closer, she could faintly see it was in fact a large stone jutting out of the mountainside. It was most certainly black and the rest of the stone was rough and went into the mountain. The air around the stone felt very different and she sensed that there was something on the other side of the stone, as though it were an opening or a door.

Holna took a step forward, she was so intrigued by the stone face that she was not mindful of her step and tripped. She stumbled up onto rock. In the last moments of daylight, she could see how the stone not only extended up into a flush face but also vertically beneath her. It was the stone itself she had tripped upon. All daylight was gone and she could not tell if the stone outcropping she now stood upon had been cut away or if it was naturally flat. Regardless, she felt that she was inside the stone.

It seemed an ideal location to spend the night, a level surface and shaded by trees. She sat down on the flattened area of stone and placed the book down in front of her. She looked down the mountainside, she could hear the snow continuing to fall. She picked up the book and moved her back to the vertical face of the stone. She brought the book under Ulh's robe and wrapped her arms around it. There was a soothing familiarity with the book close to her chest again.

Holna rested her head on the stone and felt the cold hard surface against the back of her head. She drew Ulh's robe in around her more tightly and listened to snowflakes land and strike the leaves high above her; the pitch black sounding as a continual settling, a perpetual movement towards stillness.

Holna closed her eyes and continued listening to the sound of the snowfall. The dark currents beneath her eyelids flowed as the world softened. Holna fell asleep.

> A scarred landscape
> of earth and stone,
> mountains.
>
> A dark smoke in the air.
> Flags, set high, ruffle and crack,
> spiked poles.
>
> A trench coming out of a mountain,
> narrow,
> one man deep.
>
> A great even rumbling in the distance.
>
> An army marches with a rigid and steady gait.
> Holna among them.
>
> With their rhythmic stride, they bleed along the trench vein.
> From within their pulse, another,

lower, deeper.
Holna is filled with dread.
An anxiety, a propulsion,
to leave or to hold ranks.

Holna turns, pushes through troops, no resistance, they march on.
Up the steep embankment of the trench,
clawing ground and rock.
Above the trench,
the long line of troops,
lined for miles,
and miles,
behind and beyond Holna.

The rumbling sound grows,
it fills her with euphoria,
she cannot wait to meet it.

She runs,
in opposition to the troops course.
She runs hard,
along the edge of the trench,
on the lip of the embankment.

A sharp curve,
it follows the contour of a small mountain.
Holna rounds the turn,
a blistering speed,
the obscuration of an enduring corner,
the blind of proximity.

The rumble grows on.
Troops march on, still her rapid stride,
counterflow.

A rush of heat, a lava,
thrusting through, engulfing the trench.

It consumes all,
troops and every feature, every space.
No cries or resistance,
within the hiss and pop
liquid splatter and coursing weight,
lava thickens within the trench, consumes them all.

Holna runs harder,
then leaps high,
the air whistles.
Above the trench she soars.
In her descent,
she turns, lengthens her arms,
opens her chest.

She lands flat on her back
on thick lava,
on the heavy heated flow.
The strike of her form
a crack hardening of liquid into cradling rock.
Black and dense,
it molds to her.

She flows down the trench in a warm comfort.

The world is a thick rumbling.

18.

Rain fell in the caves.

Water was all around Ulh. Multitudes of drips and drops came down upon him in the dark. They reverberated throughout the caves and he was lost in the torrent.

Ulh had crawled on all fours like a stalking animal moving through the caves listening to the spaces he occupied. He would slap his hands against the cave floor using the reverberation to guide him. He had steadily moved through varied spaces, some were open, others very tight. On a number of occasions he had hit his head, a couple of times he paused from the pain and to rest his knees.

For some time the caves had been cold but dry. Now the echoes of his hands on the rock floor of the cave had guided him to a space full of moisture, the disorienting, dripping ambience in which he now found himself. He found it difficult to hear what the slapping of his hands on the cave floor told him of the features of the space. There were hundreds, thousands, of dripping sounds all about him. He was completely lost. He was in another world and he had no way of guiding himself through it. The means that had brought him there were now impotent.

Pools, pools, he thought, as he stared into the dark. His knees were sore again and most likely bleeding. He stopped crawling and laid down on his front. He placed one hand over the other and turned his head, resting it upon his hands. Drops of water coated his back. The pools speak, they speak, they speak, his thoughts wove in with the multitude of wet pulsations.

Ulh recalled the dream-visions that had brought him to the caves. For years they came to him and they were always the same. It was a clearing in a forest, ringed by trees with lush grass and a collection of small pools of water. Inside they speak. Ulh remembered his blissful excursions into each one, their unique voices and their insights. When they came to him in his sleep, he would enter their waters. Each pool was deep and their perimeters just accommodated him. They spoke so much of the world, its sizes and depths, its strange places both exquisite and frightening; the elation and sorrow of life. He saw proportions and objects he did not understand. Immersed in the pools, he would go beyond what he saw in his mind and what the pools said so that he felt what the pools communicated. Every journey into a pool was a profound and all-absorbing experience, yet he never fully understood what they imparted and why they came to him in his sleep.

They must be crossed, across, they must be crossed as the woman did. Ulh recalled her crossing the hole on the plains. He was struck by the beauty of the event, it was a wonderful surprise. Crossing waters. He had been guided around the edge of the hole. There was a vibrant air churning from within in it and he could not help being spun by it. It was such a euphoric experience. Somehow he knew that the hole was not of the world, not of the ground, not of the sky, nor of the sea. It was a foreign space in a space.

Ulh had sensed the hole before seeing the rising land of the plains beyond the woods. He had felt its air and its motion, well before he saw it.

It was a fullness and a richness calling him. It drew him deep from within his chest. He was so excited to reach the hilltop. He had no idea what would be there, and when he saw the hole, he had so many questions about it that he could not begin to sort through them. It reminded him of the pools in his sleep but it was not the same context, this was while he was awake. To feel that sensation in his chest when he was awake was so powerful. Running up the hillside, for a moment he believed his dream world and his waking world had come together; it would be a world like no other. But what he found was an emptiness made into the world.

Ulh had sat at the hole's edge because he could feel its depth. The closest he could come to it and immerse himself in it was to orbit its edge. What emitted from the hole filled him and moved him without the use of his muscles or his thoughts. He was thrilled by the absence of knowing, he was propelled by a felt questioning.

When Ulh had stopped moving and thrust out his arms towards the hole, he had reached out to receive the depth he could not reach and the woman was the conduit. She could move through it and she could cross it, because she did not know what it was and she had no understanding of her ability to be within it.

When their hands met, Ulh felt her fear, her shock and her will to survive, but through that was the power of the mysterious space in the ground. It was a brief soothing sensation because he had let it pass through him. As the wind, as running water and as echoes, Ulh let the nature of the hole pass beyond him to where it needed to go. He could not grasp it in his mind, his heart or his body but he could feel the power of it. In that moment he only knew what to do but not why. It was an odd knowing.

Ulh's reverie of the hole was so palpable and rich that fatigue overcame him. Lying on the cave floor, he focused again on the rhythms of dripping water around him and on his body. His breath passed over his hands and across the stone. His chest pressed in against the cave floor as he inhaled; the sound of air within him was immense. With his exhale, the air rushed out and his back sunk towards the cave floor. His naked body against the cold stone, the dripping water and his breath were a familiar union, at once soothing and confusing. He laughed a little at the paradox.

Ulh fell asleep.

Ulh stood,
he was a boy,
on the deck of an immense ship.
No sails, no wood,
many bright colours,
shimmering steel.
The ship cut through water,
towered over the sea.

Many people milled about,
odd clothing, strange words.

The boat shook. It was being struck.
No reactions, no cries,
people chatted, smiled at the view.

Ulh's father appeared, went to him.
"Over here!" his father said.
They went to one side of the ship.
The boat continued to be struck,
in a regular rhythm,
a jagged pulse from the sea.

Ulh looked over the rail of the boat.
Ripples of dark,
lustering creatures,
breaching the surface of the water,
fins rising, their heads striking the metal hull,
a rolling boom echoed on and on,
throughout the ship.
It tremored and creaked,
the incessant concussive calls.

Ulh's heart bloomed open. "It was not an attack," he thought.

And then again his father spoke,
"Look!" the word flooded Ulh's mind.
His father was on the other side of the boat,
waving Ulh to come closer,
"See!" the word echoed throughout Ulh's chest.
His father's finger pointed out to sea,
it pierced the horizon,
as Tor rising.

Ulh ran to his father.
Far away, over the water was an immense creature.
Light shimmered off its robust dark skin,
its fins wafted the air.
Larger than the boat,
it floated over the sea;
it rolled from side to side;
on and on,
its fins sculpted the air,

a gentle propulsion.

Water ran off its body,
fell upon the sea as a torrential rain.
The sound of the droplets,
rippling the sea,
approached as a rising hiss.

As the droplets met,
with currents and waves,
in every direction,
without limit,
in dimension,
or in speed,
a new sound emitted from the entire ocean.

Then a new ocean.
Foreign creatures flourished,
fed on one another.
The whole world spun faster.
The whole world became empty in its richness.
The whole world was a bright dark, a black luminescence.

Another new sound.

Ulh awoke. The new sound and the new ocean receded quickly. He wanted to hold on to the memory of them both. The effort to keep them had brought Ulh to his hands and knees. He was panting. His heart began to slow from its tremendous pulse. He had come out of rest, and yet his experience had exerted him.

I have never seen my father before, Ulh thought, feeling the water of the caves beading off his back. He lay back down on the cave floor and allowed himself to regain his breath. He listened to the field of dripping water, The pools speak but only when they are met, silent until a meeting.

Ulh turned over on to his back and let the drops of water fall over his chest and face.

Pools, pools. Ulh saw the the clearing and the pools in his memory, Drown and drink, drown and drink. He was overcome with the shrill memory of the sounds as he had mixed the waters. The cave and all the sounds within it receded as he succumbed to the memory of the experience. He slumped to one side and began to shiver recalling the screaming voices filling his body. His eyes teared, more drops he could not hear. The pools themselves were very much like these caves. It was an immersion of seeking and moving that involved his whole body. Yet, unlike the caves, the pools did not lead to each other, they were separate.

When Ulh was completely immersed in a pool, all space and time were unhinged. He never felt a clear progression of time as he would float absorbed in what the pool would tell. Until a sensation of up or down would present itself. Then he would leave the pool. Leaving the pool meant leaving the dream. Although it was not like any other dream. There was a feeling of having been somewhere else.

After visiting each of the pools a number of times, Ulh began to recognize contradictions in his experiences. The differences began to vex him. He was unable to question the pools, it was always a receiving experience. And so Ulh began to wonder if he could enable the pools to communicate amongst themselves, so that they may clarify the contradictions. He began to believe that if he was to understand what they told him, it would come in their water's merging. Then in one dream, Ulh chose to mix the waters. He carried a handful at a time from one pool to another. But soon he had lost track of which he had mixed and how much water he had moved between them.

Upon his next dive into one of the pools, he was seized by a painful noise, it filled his body and assailed his mind. He felt he was falling in multiple directions simultaneously and coming apart. After that experience, Ulh never spoke the same way. The noise of the pools spilled into his waking life. He upset and terrified his community until they believed he was possessed by some evil. They attempted to silence and force out his words with the whip, but when that proved fruitless, they took his tongue and exiled him.

He hid in far off mountains, sleeping for short periods of time, fearful of being overtaken by the pools. Sometimes he would be in the midst of the pools and other times he would sleep normally. But never did he wake to who he had been. He was some mixture, some result of smeared boundaries.

Ulh turned over on to his front, Drink or drown. He slammed his fist on the cave floor to bring himself back to where he was and to push back the memory of the noise that assailed him. Want to know, need to know.

Again Ulh slammed his fist on the cave floor, there was some relief. He struck again, more relief. Then he heard his heavy breathing and soon the cave floor's cold, hard surface rose up into his body. He came up on all fours. He slapped his hand on the cave floor and listened carefully. The sound of the impact went nowhere, revealed nothing beyond or within the field of drips and drops. The collective percussion of moisture swallowed his attempt to find direction. Drink or drown.

Ulh collapsed on the cave floor. He suppressed his need to scream in frustration. He lay again with one ear pressed against the cold wet rock and fell back into memory.

Some time after Ulh had mixed the waters of the pools, he had a very different dream. He was in a deep ocean. The waters were black. He was conscious of the immeasurable depths around him and was confused as to where to go and why. Then he felt movement over his body, and currents of blue appeared. A swift rise with bubbles and waves as he was thrust upward by unknown forces. Light streamed down towards him in ripples. It was water, so much water, and he breached the surface. He shot up into the air. He continued to rise, looking down he saw a great pool. One far beyond any contemplation. It was the whole world in all directions as water. Rising higher and higher, a voice spoke, "Seek a great crossing, she waits." It was neither a man nor a woman's voice, it was deep and vast. He had never heard a voice like that before. It continued, "Seek a great crossing, across and within the world, she waits." Finally, he saw and felt the pool the voice spoke of, its dynamics and its depths. He awoke to a peculiar sound, it resonated through his body, it felt as a form with a pulsing signature.

The "she" the voice spoke of confused Ulh. It was unclear to him what it referred to: a person, the world, or the waters. Yet with such questions, the experience filled him with the need to seek answers, to journey, allowing the questions to reveal their answers.

The morning of this dream, Ulh went to the sea and stowed away on a large ship. He had to hide in different places over and over again so as not to be found by the crew. It was an easy thing to do with so much of his life having been in hiding from others.

That night, he had chosen to rest beneath the prow. Ulh watched quick shards of starlight pierce through the clouds and glimmer over the water. He listened to the rhythm of the waves hitting the side of the boat. In one quick illumination of starlight over the water's surface, he saw a small boat. At first it looked empty, then for a brief moment he saw someone in the bottom. The clouds sealed and all light was obscured. Then he heard the ship strike the small boat, overturning it, wood raking over wood. The sound itself was a current that pulled at him.

Ulh jumped into the water. He saved the person from the depths and placed them back in the small boat. It was the woman. He checked her for signs of life and she was breathing. There was nothing else in the boat; the woman had a small pack on her back and a sword strapped to her waist. He left her as she was, lying on her side, one hand over the edge of the boat. It was very dark. Ulh turned to see the great vessel as it moved on away from them. No one aboard had seen or heard the impact. He watched it take what little light it carried, its lanterns and torches softened into the dark. Soon he was alone in the small boat with the woman on the cloud-covered sea. Ulh had heard the crew say they were not far from land. He chose to wait for daylight and then set off for whatever landmark was visible.

During the night, something came to the surface. It was a large creature with a smooth round shape. It let out a sudden burst of air, a spray rose up and deepened the salt in the air. The creature came very close to the boat. Ulh could not tell its exact size but it was much larger than the boat. He watched the creature and reached out to touch it. The skin was cold, slick and smooth. The creature submerged.

Moments later, it rose again and gently bumped the boat. The creature was so gentle despite its size, that Ulh took the woman's hand draped just over the edge of the boat and stretched it out to touch the creature's skin. He ensured that her whole palm pressed against the creature. Again, the creature submerged; it did not resurface.

It was not long before first light appeared. Ulh saw a sliver of land and began rowing. He put his whole body into the effort. It was a full day of rowing before they reached land; the woman was unconscious the entire journey. At the beach, Ulh found a door on the rocks, the peculiarity of it assured him this was a powerful place. The great pool had brought them together. But the boat journey was not a complete crossing. He needed to help her successfully cross. A door, a crossing, must keep going.

Ulh's reverie energized him. Drink or drown. As he remained stretched out on the cave floor, he slapped his hand against the the wet stone. The sound was consumed by the swarming din of dripping water. He took a deep breath, his exhalation sounded over the cave floor and his breath emptied. In the pause he heard a soft even trickle in his ear that rested on the cold stone. He pressed his ear hard into the stone; there it was, a continuous flow. Within the stone, sounding apart from the drone pulses of falling water, a guiding line. There was a stream somewhere in the caves.

Ulh listened and came onto all fours. He crawled, alternating his hands so he could reach out into the dark to feel what was before him. He moved along and then again pressed his ear to the cave floor. Again, the faint rumble, the continuous line. He continued on and reached out to stone surfaces and the dark. He felt for the direction, the source of the sound which came from the cave floor. He placed his ear to the cave floor once more. The sound was growing.

Stone resonant with direction.

19.

The air trembled with birdsong.

Holna awoke and her eyes opened to warmth. Tor's light beamed through an opening in the trees and fell upon her face. She softened into the hard surface of the stone she sat upon and bathed in the warmth of the light. She relaxed a little more as she drew the book closer to her chest and wrapped Ulh's tunic tighter around herself.

Sleep was still in her eyes and so the light coming through the trees was broken into straight edges, like sheets of paper, or the hard edge of a sword. Why is that?

Holna remembered very little of her dreams but she felt that she had experienced much in her sleep. It felt the same as having run for a long time. She tried to remember images or feelings but the only palpable image was that of a liquid light, coursing and shifting. Seeing Tor's light as she did now, felt to be an odd juxtaposition. Straight light, liquid light, what is light? What is Tor? Why is it in the sky?

She recalled the fire Ulh had made the night they reached the mountains. Is that the same light? And what of the lightning? She recalled other instances of light in her life: the first time she made a fire; the burning arrows that came and killed so many; the sparks when using tinder, when sword sharpening; the light she saw when she kissed that mysterious woman during the spring rituals. What was all that light?

More light came through the branches and her eyes watered in fatigue from the brilliance. Closing her eyes, she shifted a little, feeling the stone beneath her and the flat surface of the book at her chest. "Please, for me." The head monk's voice boomed in her mind and then coursed through her body. The light lost its heat, it softened and she was in shadow.

Holna wiped the sleep from her eyes and looked around. Clouds obscured Tor. She turned and could see that she was indeed sitting in an outcropping of black stone as she had vaguely surmised the previous night. It was shale-like with long radiating lines and fissures lengthening out from where she sat. She could not tell if the surface she sat upon had been cut away or if it had happened naturally.

Holna felt a shiver. The moment of warmth that had woken her was dramatically different to the cold that now overcame her. The air had changed in her ascent of the mountain and with Tor behind clouds, the initial warmth of sunlight that had reached her receded quickly.

She stood up and backed away from the vertical face of the stone. Holna could see more of the stone's jagged lines and fissures. In them was the depth and compaction of the stone's life. Those lines were openings to its time, its journey and its dimensions.

Suddenly a glimmer of light whisked across the stone's surface. It was so brief Holna was not sure if it had actually happened or if it had been a trick of her eyes. She covered her eyes with the palms of her hands and rubbed them. A deep fatigue came into her body, her sleep had been busy and the journey was wearing on her. She was very tired and her body ached. She pushed back against the oncoming sensation and threw her hands away from her eyes to see the deep black grooves of stone.

Holna stepped off the stone and walked around it to examine the stone and see if she could reproduce the luminous effect. Nothing happened. Holna looked at the mountainside. Very little snow had fallen during the night but there was enough to have covered the trees and form a thin layer in between the trees. She looked to the sky, it was covered in clouds. If the light she had seen from the stone was because of direct sunlight or a trick of her eyes due to her fatigue, it was unlikely to happen again. Holna sighed and then laughed to herself.

She looked backed upon the course she had taken. The mountain slope descended to the plains that were a single green expanse to an obscure horizon of the thin shimmer of the sea.

Her journey had been laid by Tor and it was now concealed by the clouds. Tor was easier to gaze upon behind the clouds, a smooth and clear circle, but it still brought a discomfort to her eyes. Will this ever end? Will I go back the way I came?

Holna's thoughts held her gaze on Tor long enough for the light to hurt her eyes. She turned from Tor and looked down at her feet. Her eyes were blinded by the light that lingered in her vision. Again she put her palms up to her eyes.

The woods were quiet. As her vision cleared into the usual movement of dark in her lidded eyes, she noticed how thick and deep the quiet around her was. She began to see a light brimming at the edges of her vision. It was sharp and very active. She uncovered her eyes. Looking down, her feet came into focus and light came down on her. The clouds had opened. Holna avoided looking at Tor and turned to the stone face.

The stone exploded with light. Fragments and filaments came from all the pours and vertices of the dark stone. Holna squinted and hid her eyes, colours moved within the white radiance. This is it, this is what the head monk spoke of, "Walk with Tor, follow its path, without exception, until Tor turns to stone." It is so beautiful.

She felt the head monk's hand upon her chest where she had carried the book. Love beamed within her and she felt nowhere to send it, nowhere to receive it. The force of it within her, churning tightly, weakened her legs and she shivered, collapsing to the ground. She looked up at the stone through tear-flooded eyes and the light deepened in its beauty and splendour. The dance of light matched what was inside her.

There were foreign voices within her speaking, "I don't deserve this. Please, for me. This moment, please, for me. This time, please, for me. This beauty, please, for me. What is it, please. Why is it, for me." She did not know where the thoughts came from. They engulfed her. The thoughts, their tones and rhythms, were of voices unknown to her. And yet, they were of her. They echoed on. Growing and receding, diminishing and amplifying, as an enigmatic maelstrom from which she could not hide. They continued, "Please, for me, for me, for me." They found new places within her, seeking her out while coming from within her.

Holna let out her battle scream and it was nothing like it had ever been. Her voice swarmed the mountainside, and for her, the mountain shook, the sea she had crossed deepened, and the sky opened to let her voice pass beyond it. She was on her hands and knees, like an animal she panted.

When she regained her breath, Holna stood up and removed her sword. It dropped to the ground but she never heard the impact.

Holna walked to the stone. As she did, her shadow fell over its deep-lined pores but it did not block the light coming from the stone. Just as what she felt inside was open and unobscured, luminous gestures never waned in their radiant expression from the stone. She brought the book to the middle of her chest with one hand and placed her other hand on the cold stone.

Holna's palm was fully extended. The subtle lines of her skin met the lined veins of the stone. The twists and ripples of her palm lines aligned with the vertical fissures of the stone that ran up to the sky and into the mountain. The touch of the stone became smooth. Her fingers tightened around the wax that held the book.

Holna waited, something was emerging within her. There was a shape, a form moving, "Me." It repeated and grew in its dimensions and depths. Holna allowed it to fill her. With its presence came a knowing. She pushed her hand against the stone. Beneath one of her fingers the wax that enveloped the book cracked into a sliver opening. The sound thundered down out of the mountain and up into the sky.

The world shook.

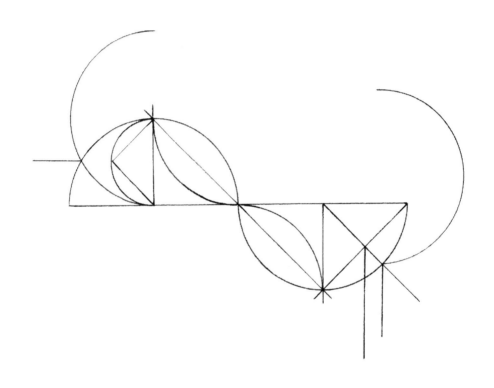

20.

A voice deep within the stone sang.

Ulh had patiently followed the tuned tremor reverberating through the rock. Bringing his ear to the cave floor, he listened for the faint rumble within the stone as dripping water fell all around him. Listening for any change in the sound to guide him, he had proceeded through the dark, reaching out to find the stream of water that called to him. Ulh had moved through the field of drips and drops with no awareness of distance from place to place or the passage of time. His journey had been only in that faint line of the rumbling contour from out of the rock.

"Seek a great crossing, across and within the world." He recalled the words as he felt the voice that had spoken and the peculiar sound that had resonated through his body.

There had been moments when he felt a frustration, when he was a little maddened with the barrage of drops of water, when the sound in the stone he followed seemed so impersonal or as a trap cultivating a disillusionment in his mind. A number of times he had stopped and sat on the cave floor to think. Why do the pools speak? Why drink, why drown? Crossing and crossing. Across.

It was in one of these pauses of frustration that he had sighed to himself and a faint growling hum emerged from him. The rumbling sensation came from his throat and his chest. It was soothing. He rested his head on the cave floor and his ear stung a little from his repeated listenings. There again was the faint rumble in the stone, and with it, he growled, stimulating his throat and heart as he had when he first sighed. The sensation was uplifting. He proceeded on in this way seeking the source of the distant tuned tremor within the stone. It was a unique dialogue.

The drips and drops never subsided, but with his focus within the cave floor, the dripping waters lost their potency to fluster him as a single unified field. The faint line guiding Ulh as it grew in intensity. And then with an outstretched hand, dotted by drops of cold water, Ulh felt what he had been listening to, his fingers dipped into a vein of coursing water. He euphorically seized upon it with the other hand. His breath quickened in exhilaration of the line, a sharp contrast to the interminable points of water that had been striking him above. His fingers ran along the the length of the moving line of water. Then, with his hands in the thin, cool, running channel, he followed its course. It was not long before it deepened and broadened.

Soon it became an ample stream, its dynamics shimmering, echoing in the shifting dimensions of the dark caves. Ulh crawled in the gently flowing stream. His eyes caught luminous slivers on the surface of the water he followed. He looked up and hanging before him was a thin fragment of light. He continued moving through the running water as the light grew.

The light sharpened and emerged out of the dark as an opening. Ulh stood up, using the cave walls for support and stepped into an immense chamber. At its center was a sharp shaft of light coming down from an opening high above. Hanging down from the opening was a root system which intertwined into long pointed extensions of stone. They appeared to have grown together. Looking around, Ulh saw similar stone formations with smooth rounded sides coming to points that reached toward the cave ceiling.

As his eyes adjusted to the light, Ulh could see that the cave floor was pooled with water. Toward its centre the rock floor rounded up to where the shaft of light fell upon a large stone with a flat top. All the stone of the chamber floor was slick with moisture and shimmered. Beneath that reflective coating were colourations: greens, dark blues, browns, greys and blacks that swirled out from the flat stone at the top. The cave walls were rounded and curved away from Ulh into an immense infinite darkness.

Ulh proceeded into the chamber. He waded slowly through the water as it came to his knees. Pools, pools, drink or drown, drink and drown, cross, seek a great crossing. The sounds of the water rose gently from the surface and were carried out into the great expanse of the chamber. One step after another, the water became shallower as the reverberances grew. When the water came to Ulh's ankles, the dark of the water revealed the texture of the stone beneath it. The light from the opening above reflected on the water and concentric luminous curves emanated from his his ankles.

Ulh soon reached areas of the rounded stone floor that were dry amid currents of shallow water. He cautiously picked his way from dry point to dry point. Each dry area was a deep black, while the waters contained swirling colours. At times, Ulh could see the grains of earth, sand and other particles within the water trails. He was picking his way through the dynamics of the place, its age and its history. Eventually, the trails of water joined and the smooth, rounded cave floor was all slick with moisture. To avoid slipping, Ulh went down on his hands and knees and crawled to reach where the light cast directly on the hanging roots and the even-topped stone.

Directly under the opening in the chamber ceiling, Ulh looked up. The edges of the opening were rough and met with the smooth curve of the long root system that descended, twisting and binding itself to the stone formations that became the even topped stone. With the root and smooth stone pillaring to one side, the large flat stone looked very much like a throne.

Ulh sat on the large even-topped stone directly within the shaft of light and crossed his legs. The entrance was in front of him, the roots and limestone pillar to his right, and behind him was the black void of the chamber. The multi-coloured swirls on the chamber floor radiated beyond him. They revealed the history of the flow of water. From this position he felt at the center of a great primordial mass. He could see where he had crawled and disturbed the contours of colour and water. Some parts had already begun to reassert the trajectories he had altered, while other portions seemed forever changed.

Ulh thought of the pools in his sleep and how he had mixed the waters. He was overcome with the depth of the importance of what he had just done to the chamber floor. Every step and movement he had made through the caves had changed things in ways he could not comprehend. His body was filled with a growing tremor. Pools, the pools, the pools are crossing. Drink or drown, drink and drown. The pools, they are crossing. Seek a great crossing. He felt the painful noise when he had crossed the waters of the pools in his dreams.

He turned away from the swirls and patterns on the cave floor and looked out to the great void of the chamber. Looking to those invisible depths, the painful noise continued within him. Growing and rippling, it magnified into a self-cycling wave, it exerted more and more motion. He was on the point of suppressing it, when his breath became heavy and he succumbed to the discomfort within. All he could do was listen, just as he had for the faint line within the cave floor seeking direction from a crossing. A current of sound appeared within him, it was the voice that had spoken of the crossing and it was accompanied with the peculiar sound that had resonated through his body.

Ulh opened his mouth and forced sound. It strained his throat and his jaw as he uttered rough, gurgled and stuttered noises so different from the words and images in his mind. As they moved throughout the chamber they became a smooth ripple. They developed into expanding and lengthening textures displacing and transforming the depths of the chamber.

From above, a gust of air came through the opening. It howled into the chamber and merged with the reverberance of Ulh's voice. They grew together, increasing in size and intensity as they sounded throughout the chamber, modifying its sea of dark.

The chamber resonated in every dimension with and within Ulh. They reverberated one another. It was an accompaniment. It was an evolution.

All was sound.

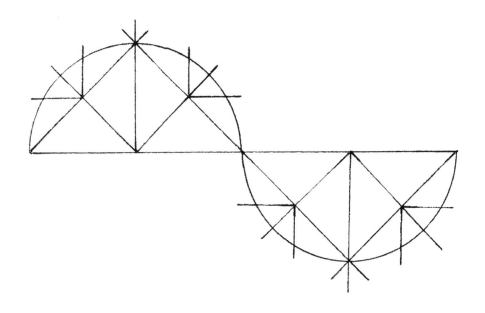

Acknowledgements

I began "The Books of Magra" almost twenty years ago. It has always been about the intention to inspire and cultivate the exploration of consciousness, and certainly this intention has greatly affected my own personal journey. However, it would not have been possible without a number of people that I have been blessed to have in my life both professionally and personally.

First, I would like to thank my parents for their endless love and support.

I would like to thank Daniel Tibbits, for his humour, creativity and love. I do not have words for what having you in my life means to me.

I would like to thank Michelle Tibbits who has always been a true friend, you have been like the big sister I never had.

I would like to thank David Gross who has aided me time and time again in so many ways, what I have learned and manifested because of your support is incalculable and ineffable.

I would like to thank Jennifer Honyara for her support and continually reminding me that life is a playground.

I would like to thank my friends and creative peers, sharing in your respective journeys has been profoundly moving and important to me.

I would like to thank Joanne Madeley and Arina Tanase for their insightful views that helped mold the early stages of this manuscript.

Finally, I would like to thank Sylvia Taylor for her meticulous and passionate editing, which not only improved the final product but also helped me to be a better writer.

About the Author

Joël Tibbits is a Vancouver-based composer, sound designer and writer.

At an early age, he was intrigued by sound, an attraction that began with his father's record collection and lead to his study of music composition. In addition to this profound fascination with sound, he was equally drawn to mysticism, mythology and science. This cocktail of interests took him on to further studies of the martial arts, yoga, meditation and bioenergetic modalities.

Over the years, he has initiated several innovative projects focusing on altered states of consciousness and healing through music and sound. His music, writing, classes and workshops, focus on fostering a deeper understanding of consciousness, self-knowledge, creativity and participatory relationship.

Made in the USA
Lexington, KY
30 September 2018